MITZI MAL...

Mitzi got out of bed and went over to her bookshelf. She reached behind an old collection of magazines and pulled out the envelope she'd stashed there. Then, she counted her money.

It wasn't enough. She'd planned on saving up more than two hundred dollars for her trip to New York. She wasn't even close.

But it would have to do. She couldn't wait any longer.

Maddie . . .

What if she told Maddie that she couldn't come to work for a few days? She could say she was sick . . . or that a family emergency had come up.

But lying to Maddie didn't seem fair, after she had been so nice and everything. And somehow, Mitzi didn't think she could bring herself to look Maddie in the eye and tell a lie. No, Maddie wasn't someone you lied to.

The time had come for Mitzi's plan to be put into action.

She would run away on Sunday night. She would write Maddie a letter telling her the whole story, and she'd mail it on Saturday so it would arrive on Monday.

Since she wouldn't have enough money for a motel, maybe she could sleep in the Port Authority Bus Terminal. There must be a bench in there. And if there wasn't one, she could just sleep on the floor. It was only for a few nights.

Mitzi crawled back into bed.

Then she turned off the light and lay awake in the dark, planning.

MITZI MALLOY
AND THE
ANYTHING-BUT-HEAVENLY
SUMMER

WENDY CORSI STAUB

Z·FAVE
KENSINGTON PUBLISHING CORP.

For the Pucci Family—
Aunt Mickey, Uncle Ron, Katie, Michael, &
Chrissy . . .
For my husband, Mark . . .
And in memory of a special angel, Uncle "Bertie"—
Albert Ricotta
June 8, 1940—November 3, 1948

Z*FAVE BOOKS are published by

Kensington Publishing Corp.
850 Third Avenue
New York, NY 10022

Z*FAVE and the Z*FAVE logo Reg. U.S. Pat. & TM Off.

First Printing: June, 1995

Printed in the United States of America

Prologue

SILVER FALLS REGISTER, JUNE 12, 1983

FREAK ACCIDENT KILLS FOUR AT ADVENTURELAND

Four Silver Falls High School seniors were fatally injured when an amusement park ride malfunctioned during a class outing at Adventureland amusement park in Keaton.

According to John A. Calzone, spokesperson for Adventureland, the accident occurred just past nine last evening, and involved the Whirling Twirl-a-Curl ride, a corkscrew-shaped roller coaster contraption that revolves on a base and is fitted with an eight-car train. "We are always concerned with safety here at Adventureland," Calzone stated. "The Whirling Twirl-a-Curl is equipped with several protective features, including a metal harness bar that keeps riders in their seats when the ride goes upside down. Apparently, somehow, something went wrong."

All four victims were riding in the last car of the train. The ride had been in motion for over a minute, says operator Marvin "Stitch" Melvin, when he heard a clanging noise and observed a problem with the rear car, which was suspended upside-down twenty-two feet in the air. The safety harness had evidently malfunctioned, and the passengers were thrown from the car. All four received massive internal injuries.

Madeline Parpelli, 17, of Silver Falls, was pronounced dead at the scene. The other victims, who were taken to Keaton General Hospital and later died there, were Nathan Oakley, 18; Thea Caruthers, 18; and Bryan O'Brock, 18, all of Silver Falls. A memorial service will be held tomorrow evening at the Silver Falls High School auditorium at seven o'clock.

The Whirling Twirl-a-Curl has been shut down indefinitely, and an investigation into the accident is continuing.

(Obituaries on page 4-B)

"Hey, Nathan, want a cookie?" Madeline asked with her mouth full of chewy chocolate chip.

"No, thanks," he said, glancing up from the baseball magazine he was reading. "How many of those are you going to eat?"

"As many as I want—why not? I never get full, and I never get fat!" she announced jubilantly, reaching into the bag again. "I always *knew* heaven would be like this."

"This isn't heaven, Maddie—it's, like, purgatory or something," Thea reminded her. She was lounging nearby on an enormous overstuffed couch, buffing her nails. "And when you *do* finally make it to heaven one of these days, you'd better hope that it's more than an all-you-can-eat snack bar."

Maddie shrugged and bit into another cookie, this one buttery and rich, with cinnamon-sugar crystals sprinkled over the top. She decided the next one she ate would be an icing-covered bonbon with a maraschino cherry in the middle, knowing all she had to do was reach into the bag, and presto! The cookie she'd conjured mentally would be there. They always were. And after the bonbon, she'd try . . .

"Hey, guys," Bryan said, appearing suddenly in front of them.

Maddie wondered if she'd ever get used to the way people popped in and out all the time around this place. At least, she'd finally figured out how to do it herself—just close your eyes and concentrate on where you wanted to go. Not that there were many choices.

Ever since the four of them had arrived the other day—or had it been last month? It was so hard to tell—they'd been restricted to this area, the Holding Gardens.

According to Celeste, they had to wait here until they received their assignments, which could be any minute—or any day—now. Celeste, who always wore a khaki uniform and a badge that said "Guide," had been waiting for Maddie when she'd first straggled through the garden gates, bewildered, vaguely reluctant, but strangely euphoric, too.

The smiling, golden-haired beauty had instantly thrown her arms around Maddie and said, "Welcome!"

And that had evaporated Maddie's last lingering inkling to go back.

Besides, the others had arrived right behind her. Nathan Oakley, the shy next-door neighbor she'd had a crush on since kindergarten; pretty but self-centered Thea Caruthers, her best friend on earth (and here, too); and Bryan O'Brock, Thea's latest boyfriend—who was her usual dark and dangerous, walk-on-the-wild-side type.

The Holding Gardens were lush and sun-dappled, with fountains and chirping birds and even a swimming pool. There were other people here, too—some who kept to themselves, snoozing and lounging, and others who mingled in groups, talking and joking around as if this were a summer barbecue in someone's yard.

There were people of all races, speaking dozens of different languages. But Maddie had noticed that everyone had one thing in common—age. No one appeared to be younger than their late teens, or older than their early thirties. It was like a giant MTV-Generation convention in the sky.

If they even *were* in the sky. Who could tell?

All Maddie knew was that one minute, she'd been scared out of her wits and about to barf on that stupid Whirling Twirl-a-Curl ride she'd gone on to impress Nathan, and the next minute, she'd been dreamily walking toward the gleaming garden gates, where Celeste stood beckoning her.

"Hey, Maddie," Bryan said, breaking into her reverie. He shoved his dark, too-long (in Maddie's opinion) hair off his face and held up a piece of paper. "I just saw Celeste, and she said for me to give you this."

She popped the rest of the sugar cookie into her mouth, licked her fingers, and took it. "What is it?"

Bryan shrugged and stood waiting, his hands deep in his jeans pockets in his usual slouchy stance. Nathan took a few steps closer, and Thea propped herself up on her elbows to watch as Maddie unfolded the paper and scanned the message there.

It was as if they all knew what was about to happen.

Maddie's first thought was how amazing it was that someone had taken the time to letter the note in swirling, perfect calligraphy—unbelievably classy, like everything else around here.

Her second thought was *This is it.*

Her third thought was *I need that bonbon now,* and she reached into the bag and popped it into her mouth, whole.

"Wow," Nathan said, reading over her shoulder.

"What?" Thea asked, tossing her long, dark hair and standing up to join them. "What does it say?"

Maddie tried speak but was muffled by the cookie she was chewing. She jabbed Nathan in the ribs and motioned for him to fill Bryan and Thea in.

He cleared his throat. "It says Maddie has to report to the gates immediately to receive her assignment."

"Huh," Bryan said cryptically.

"You'd better hustle," Thea advised, flopping back into her chair again.

Maddie nodded, swallowed the last of her cookie, and looked at Nathan. "I don't know if I'm ready."

"Of course you're ready. Go on. You basically know what you have to do. Celeste told us everything in orientation."

"I know, but . . . what about you guys?"

"We'll probably be getting our assignments any minute now, too," Thea told her.

"Yeah, and the sooner we all get this guardian angel stint out of the way, the sooner we earn our wings and blow this popsicle stand," Bryan said.

"Yeah, heaven, here we come," Nathan said, nodding and giving Maddie a light punch in the arm. "Go for it, Maddie."

"Right," she said, smiling weakly. "I'm going."

She took a deep breath, gave a little wave, and started for the gates, still gripping the bottomless bag of cookies.

When she reached her destination, she found Celeste waiting for her.

"Madeline," the girl said warmly, "are you ready?"

She nodded. "I think so."

"Good. Let me review what's going to happen before I turn you over to Justin."

"Who's Justin?"

Celeste flashed a small, secret smile. "You'll see. Now, you remember our orientation session, where we covered the basics?"

"Yup," Maddie said, nodding again. "I remember."

"Good. Then you are aware that everyone here in the Holding Gardens has one thing in common—you've all been called away from your preliminary earthbound assignments relatively early. That means you need to complete the program by an alternate means."

Mentally, Maddie translated what Celeste was saying into simpler terms. The *preliminary earthbound assignment* was human life. The *program* referred to the stages that led from life on earth to eternity in heaven. Maddie had figured out that it was sort of like you had to serve time before you got your reward. And the *alternate means* referred to the assignment Maddie was about to receive.

She was about to become someone's guardian angel.

"Are you ready, then, Maddie?" Celeste asked.

"Ready, willing, and able," Maddie said, then gulped and added, "I hope."

"Good." Celeste took her arm and together they stepped through the gates.

Ever since she'd arrived in the Gardens, Maddie had been trying to remember what she had seen just before she'd been greeted by Celeste that night. But all she could remember was a bright light shining straight ahead, where Celeste was beckoning her from the gates.

Now as she stepped over the threshold onto the other side again, she looked around curiously. She didn't remember any of this.

The funny thing was, it looked just like heaven always did in the movies—just a lot of nothingness, with misty, wispy clouds floating around. Not that this *was* heaven.

Heaven, she knew by now, was nearby but elusive. Celeste had been mysterious whenever anyone had asked her a question about it. All she ever said was, "You'll find out."

Maddie was bursting with curiosity. The Holding Gardens seemed like paradise, what with those magical bottomless bags of cookies and everything. Could heaven be even better? It was hard to imagine that was possible.

"Justin?" Celeste called, peering into the mist.

Instantly, a man appeared in front of them. He was youngish—maybe in his early twenties—and great-looking. Better-looking, even, than Nathan, Maddie decided.

Justin had dark hair, chiseled features, and a muscular build. He was wearing baggy jeans, a sweatshirt, and a backward baseball cap. He looked vaguely familiar. Where had Maddie seen him before?

"Madeline Parpelli," he said, grinning at her and then hugging her. "I've been waiting for you."

"You have?" she asked, caught off guard by the hug. She was careful not to let him crush her bag of cookies.

"Did you tell her who I am, Celeste?" Justin asked.

"Not yet."

"I'll tell her, then. Unless she wants to guess?" He looked expectantly at Maddie.

"I have no idea," she said, shaking her head.

"Then I'll clue you in. I'm *your* guardian angel."

"You're kidding." She stared at him.

He didn't look like any angel she'd ever imagined. But then, she supposed, neither did she. And she was about to become one, too, right?

This was definitely a strange place.

"I was assigned to you the day you were born—October 29, 1966. I was always with you after that, taking care of you."

"Yeah?" she asked dryly. "Then where were you that night at Adventureland when I fell head first off the Whirling Twirl-a-Curl?"

He winced slightly. "Hey, sorry about that. But when your time's up, Maddie, your time's up. That had been decided long before you went to Adventureland. And my job was to take care of you up until that point."

"You mean I would have been dead sooner if you hadn't come to my rescue?"

He and Celeste exchanged a glance, and then he shrugged. "Something like that. But actually, my job wasn't just to save you from an untimely end—it was to help you over some rough spots. Like, remember that day back in eighth grade when Toby Reynolds sang "I don't want her, you can have her, she's too fat for me" to you during coed gym class?"

Maddie shifted uncomfortably. "Yeah."

"Well, remember how you ran home crying and begged God to make you skinny?"

"Yeah."

Justin shrugged. "You asked for help, and you got it. I helped you lose all that baby fat."

Maddie looked doubtfully at him. "Yeah, right. No offense, but I dieted and exercised like crazy to get rid of that weight. You can't tell me that you, like, waved your magic wand or something and poof! The blubber magically melted away."

"Of course not. But you needed strength, and I sort of nudged you along in that department. Ultimately, it was up to you."

"Hmm." Maddie watched him for a moment, then shrugged and looked over at Celeste.

As if on cue, the guide smiled, stepped forward, and gave her a quick squeeze, and said, "I've got to get back now, Maddie. Good luck."

"Wait—will I see you again?"

"Sure. You'll do whatever you want . . . *after* you've earned those wings. I'll be around. See you, Maddie." With that, she drifted back to the gates and disappeared inside.

Maddie turned back to Justin. "So, what's the deal here? Did you earn your wings by helping me?"

"Yup."

"Where are they?" she asked, peering over his shoulder.

"My wings? Oh, that's just a figure of speech. It just means that you've achieved the ultimate goal—that you've been rewarded with access to heaven for all eternity."

"So wings are kind of like an unlimited free pass?"

He grinned. "Kind of."

"Where *is* heaven?" she asked, looking around. But all she could make out was mist, mist, and more mist.

"You'll see."

"What's it like there?"

"It's indescribable." Justin sighed and looked blissful for a moment, then became all business again. "You'll have to find out for yourself."

"Are you sure I'll be able to do that?"

"I'm sure. But first, you have a job to take care of. Someone is about to be born in a little town called Somerset in upstate New York. She's going to need you."

"But what can I do for her?"

"You'll see. And I'll help you. Come on, let's go see what's going on."

Maddie hesitated only a moment. And in that moment, a sound drifted to her ears. It was faint, and yet distinct.

A baby crying.

Her heart fluttered in response, and a smile touched Maddie's lips.

"All right, let's go." Clutching her bag of cookies with one hand and Justin's arm with the other, Maddie set out to see what was up with this guardian angel deal.

Chapter One

"Yo, Millicent, what's up with the giant box?"

Mitzi Malloy stopped walking and glanced up from the sidewalk to see that nosy, two-years-younger Rascal Timmons had pulled up alongside her on his bike.

"Nothing's up with the box, *Hulbert*," she said, putting the emphasis on the given name she knew he hated. *An eye for an eye,* she thought grimly. She'd never forgive her brother Benjie for telling Rascal that her own real name was Millicent. She gripped the box tightly against her stomach and said shortly, "I'm carrying some stuff home, that's all, *Hulbert*."

She started walking again.

"Hey, don't call me that," he said, giving his bike a one-footed pedal that allowed him to coast alongside her at the curb. "What kind of stuff?"

"Don't call me Millicent, and it's none of your business."

"Sheesh! *Someone*'s in a rotten mood," Rascal said, shaking his head and pedaling on down the street toward his house, which was kitty-corner across the street from the Malloys'.

Mitzi continued walking, concentrating on the sidewalk again. She'd made a deal with herself. If she didn't step on a single crack the whole way from Somerset Middle School on Lymon Avenue to her house on Rebecca Court, her father would come home for dinner on time tonight, and her mother would be in a good mood.

Only half a block to go.

Good, because this box was starting to feel really heavy. Inside was as much clutter from her locker as she could carry. She'd left twice as much more behind, and it would be a miracle if she got all of it home without hiring a U-Haul or something. She only had two more days before school would be out for the summer.

No one ever said you weren't a pack rat, she told herself, stopping for a second between sidewalk cracks to shift the box's weight again.

No, she wasn't the type of person who could blithely toss everything into the garbage, like her best friend Nikki Basil had done. But then Nikki's locker hadn't been as jam-packed as Mitzi's was.

How had she accumulated so much stuff since last September? Used-up spiral notebooks, old copies of *Sassy* and *Seventeen*, gym socks and mittens (all of them singles), tubes of lint-covered lip-gloss that were missing their caps, read and unread paperback books, even the Counting Crows CD she'd borrowed from Nikki over Christmas vacation and thought she'd lost.

Christmas. The memory of it made Mitzi's mood shift instantly from dark to black.

The day itself had started out fine. Snow and church and presents and everything. Mitzi's brothers had been all psyched about their new Super Nintendo game, and she had been thrilled to unwrap the leather jacket she'd coveted for months. Even her parents had seemed pleased with the gifts they'd received from each other—for a change.

Then it started.

The fighting.

It went on until her mother ran into the bathroom crying and her father slammed out of the house muttering under his breath.

And Christmas had been ruined.

"Hey, Mitzi!" someone called from somewhere above, interrupting her dismal thoughts. "Check this out!"

She looked up to see her ten-year-old brother dangling upside-down from a tree branch by his knees.

"Benjie, what the heck are you doing?" she shouted. "Get down from there before you fall and crack your head open."

He stuck his tongue out at her and waved his arms around, still dangling.

Mitzi sighed and glanced at the driveway in front of the next house up to see if her mother's car was there yet. Nope, still at work. Figured. Benjie only performed his death-defying feats when their parents weren't around to witness them. He wanted to be a movie stunt man when he grew up.

"Whoa! I'm falling!" Benjie announced, waving his arms wildly just as Mitzi started walking again.

"Benjie!" she shrieked, and then realized he was faking.

He cracked up and stuck his tongue out again.

"Brat!" Mitzi called, and started striding toward the house.

Too late, she remembered the deal she'd made with herself.

She looked down just in time to see her Nike landing smack-dab in the middle of a giant sidewalk crack.

"Hello, Suzette?" Mitzi heard her mother say in a fake-pleasant tone into the telephone in the next room. "Yes, hi, how are you? Good. Is Will still there?"

Suzette, Mitzi knew, was her father's secretary, who always smelled like vanilla and who gave Mitzi and her brothers bubblegum or suckers whenever they came into the office.

Will, of course, was Mitzi's father, William J. Malloy, who was a pretty good dad but apparently a lousy husband. At least, that was what Mitzi's mother, Carol Malloy, had been saying lately—to his face and behind his back.

"He just left?" Mitzi's mother sighed heavily in the next room. "All right, fine. Thanks. Goodb—you, too. We will. Yes, soon. 'Bye."

Mitzi heard her mother plunk the phone down and curse under her breath.

Benjie, who was sitting across the table from Mitzi, caught her eye and rolled his. Then he went back to pretending to read the comic book he'd propped in the empty plate in front of him. Mitzi knew he was probably as distracted as she was—and bracing for what was sure to happen when her father walked in the door.

Next to Benjie sat Max, six years old and oblivious to everything but the television set that droned on the kitchen counter a few feet away. It was only the evening news, but Max was always transfixed by anything that happened to be on the tube.

Lucky Max, Mitzi thought, too young to realize what was happening around here.

What *was* happening around here?

Mitzi wasn't sure. All she knew was that her parents had been fighting constantly for months now—maybe years. She couldn't remember when it had gotten bad. Sometimes, she felt like it wasn't so long ago that her parents had laughed and teased each other, or even kissed when they thought no one was watching.

Other times, she felt like it had been ages since they'd done anything but scream at each other.

Now, her mother stalked back into the kitchen and went over to the sink, not looking at Mitzi or her brothers. She was still wearing her work clothes—a navy blue floral print dress and black pumps. People were always telling Mitzi she looked like her mom, which wasn't a bad thing. They both had the same shoulder-length, wavy black hair and the same sparkly, wide-set dark brown eyes and rosy cheeks.

And lately, Mitzi was growing to be more like her mom in other ways, too. For one thing, she was almost the same height now—five foot three. And she had started wearing a bra a few months ago, too, though she had a ways to go before she caught up to her mother in *that* department.

At the sink, Mrs. Malloy turned on the water

and took a glass out of the cupboard, then stood holding the glass and letting the water run, just staring vacantly out the window above the sink.

Benjie peered at her over the top of his comic book, then raised an eyebrow at Mitzi, who shrugged to show him it was no big deal—everything was fine. Yeah, right.

She glanced at her Swatch and saw that it was almost seven o'clock. In the old days—the *good* old days—they used to eat supper by six. Now her dad rarely came home before seven, even though he was always promising her mom that he would.

Just this morning, Mitzi recalled, he had sworn he'd be home by six-fifteen at the latest because her mom had to go to some board meeting tonight at the local hospital.

But here they were as usual, waiting for Mr. Malloy to show up, while the stupid tuna casserole dried out in the oven.

Mitzi snuck a peek at her mother and saw that she had set the glass down on the counter. The water was still running, though.

"Uh, Mom?" Benjie said after a minute. "You're not supposed to waste water like that. There's a shortage."

Mitzi glared at her brother.

Her mother just looked startled and turned off the faucet, mumbling, "Sorry, I forgot."

Then her head snapped up as a car came rolling into the driveway.

"Dad's home," Benjie said helpfully.

Mitzi shot him another look, one that said, *will you please shut your big mouth?*

Benjie sent a look back that said, *make me.*

"Daddy?" Max asked happily, turning around, momentarily distracted from the TV.

Mitzi's mother glanced absently at the three of them, then went over to stand by the mudroom as a car door slammed outside.

Please let this blow over, Mitzi thought, trying to focus on the television newscaster, who was saying something boring about something boring.

Footsteps sounded on the back deck.

Mitzi's dad opened the door and stepped into the mudroom, looking weary, carrying his briefcase and wearing a dark suit.

"Don't even start with me," was the first thing he said when he saw his wife waiting by the door.

"Don't start with you?" she repeated. "Don't start with you?"

Her voice grew more shrill with every word.

Mitzi clenched her teeth and stared at the television.

"Why shouldn't I start with you?" her mother demanded. "You know I have to be at a meeting in"—she checked her watch—"twenty minutes.

You promised you'd be here so we could eat on time for a change. You *promised!* Where were you?"

"I was working, Carol," Mitzi's father said in a sarcastic tone. "You seem to be under the impression that I can just come and go when I feel like it. Something came up, and I had to—"

"Something *always* comes up!" Mitzi's mother screeched.

She went on then, hollering, and Mitzi's father hollered back. Mitzi tuned them out for as long as she could, focusing on the television anchorman, who seemed as though he'd never raised his voice or been late for dinner in his life.

Finally, when Mitzi couldn't stand it any longer, she jumped up and ran toward her bedroom, pounding up the stairs as loudly as she could to drown out the angry voices in the kitchen.

Chapter Two

"Don't tell me you're actually going to *save* that thing," said a voice behind Mitzi.

She turned to see her friend Nikki Basil standing there, wrinkling her nose at the object Mitzi had been about to toss into the bag on the floor in front of her locker.

"Of course I'm saving it," Mitzi said, holding it up. It was an orange stuck with cloves—a pomander, the substitute art teacher had called it. It was supposed to be some kind of natural air freshener.

"I threw mine away a few days after we made them. It rotted and stunk," Nikki said, tossing her long reddish-blond hair over her shoulder.

"You probably didn't do it right, then."

"Probably not. Are you almost done with that, or should I start walking without you?"

Mitzi glanced into her open locker, which

was—finally—almost bare. All that remained were a stack of paperbacks and a few magazine cutouts and photos she'd taped inside the door last September.

"Almost done," she said, picking up the books and dumping them into the bag. "Help me take down those pictures, and then we'll go."

"Good. Because I still have a lot of packing to do."

"Don't remind me." Mitzi didn't want to think about the fact that Nikki was leaving first thing in the morning for some horseback riding camp up in the hills somewhere in Connecticut.

She knew Nikki was psyched about going— she'd begged her parents to send her for the past few years. Nikki was crazy about horses. She planned to move out west someday and live on a ranch.

"What am I going to do all summer without you?" Mitzi grumbled, trying to remove her favorite picture of Ethan Hawke from her locker door without ripping it. "I kind of wish school wasn't over."

"What are you, nuts?"

"No, it's just that . . . I don't know, I have a feeling this summer is going to stink."

"I have a feeling this summer is going to be excellent."

"That's cause you're going away to some

great camp while I have to stay here in Somerset with my stupid brothers and stupid Rascal Timmons and—'' She broke off, not wanting to add the rest: *and my stupid parents who are at each other's throats day and night.*

For some reason, she hadn't told Nikki what had been going on around her house lately. Which was strange, because she usually told Nikki everything.

But this was different from having a crush on Kevin Dirkwood or being worried that she was going to get her period for the first time during school or while wearing white jeans.

The situation with her parents was something Mitzi didn't want to talk about with anyone.

And maybe if she didn't talk about it, it would go away.

Things were looking up.

Way up.

In fact, for the first time in weeks, Mitzi felt like everything was going to be all right. Like her parents had just been going through some crazy phase—maybe caused by too much stress at work, or whatever.

Right now, things were definitely back to normal. They were going out to dinner together, all five of them, to Captain Bob's Burger and Brew. That happened to be Mitzi and her brothers' fa-

vorite restaurant in Somerset. It happened to be
the place where the Malloys had always gone to
celebrate special occasions, like a birthday or a
round of good report cards. But they hadn't
been here in months now—almost a year, Mitzi
realized. The last time had been after she'd
passed the intermediate swimming test last August.

She didn't know whose idea it had been to
come here tonight to celebrate the last day of
school—her mother's or her father's. It didn't
matter. What mattered was that her father had
been home from work on time, and he and her
mother hadn't fought once during the drive
over.

Now, both of Mitzi's parents smiled and nodded as the hostess came over and said, "Table
for five? Is nonsmoking all right?"

She escorted them through the crowded dining area to a large round table. Benjie and Max
dove into chairs, and Mitzi was pulling hers out
when she heard her father say to the hostess,
"Um, miss, is there any chance of getting a
booth?"

That was odd. Mitzi and her brothers usually
wanted to sit in the booths, which had old-fashioned miniature built-in jukeboxes. But their
parents always insisted on a table. They thought
the jukeboxes were too big a distraction.

The hostess glanced around the dining room

and said, "Yes, it looks like a booth just opened up over there, if you don't mind waiting a minute while we set it up for you."

"That would be great," Mitzi's mother said, looking—relieved?

Mitzi and Benjie exchanged a glance, stood up, and stepped away from the table. Their dad scooped Max up and tickled him, the way he always used to before he and their mom had started arguing so much.

Mitzi caught her mom watching and tried to read the expression on her face. She seemed a little wistful. Maybe she missed the good old days, too. Maybe she was just as glad as Mitzi was that they were acting like a family again, out to dinner at Captain Bob's.

Moments later, the five of them were seated in a big high-backed booth by the window, Benjie and Mr. Malloy on one side, Mitzi, Max, and Mrs. Malloy on the other. Mitzi and Benjie reached simultaneously for the knob that turned the jukebox selections and jostled each other's hands for control. Max tried to grab for it, too, but his little arm was too short.

"Come on, you guys," their father said, but he didn't sound angry, the way he usually did when they fought over the jukebox. "I'll tell you what. I'll give everyone a couple of quarters and you each get to pick some songs." He reached into his pocket and started doling out change.

That was odd, Mitzi thought, accepting the four quarters he handed her. She looked at her mother, who was wearing a small, odd little smile.

"I get to choose first," Benjie said, and promptly dropped his quarters into the slot.

Mitzi didn't bother to argue, and moved her hand off the selection knob. She was getting a funny feeling in the pit of her stomach.

"Hey, they took my favorite song off the juke-box!" Benjie said, flipping through the selections for the zillionth time.

"Good," Mitzi said. She hated that song.

"Pick another one, Ben," Mr. Malloy said.

"I don't want another song. I want *that* song," he grumbled.

Mitzi pretended to concentrate on reading her menu, even though she always ordered the exact same thing at Captain Bob's—chili with cheese, potato skins with bacon, and a strawberry milkshake.

When the waitress, a pretty, blond-ponytailed high school girl, came to take their order, though, she told Mitzi, "Sorry, we don't have strawberry milkshakes anymore."

"You don't?" Mitzi frowned and picked up her menu again. Sure enough, the milkshake section was missing. In fact, the whole menu was different. The chili and skins were both listed in a different spot. She hadn't even noticed. "I'll just have a ginger ale, then," she said, closing the menu and handing it to the waitress.

And when Benjie ordered his usual selection, a burger deluxe with onion rings on the side, the waitress said, "Sorry, we don't have onion rings anymore."

"How come?" Benjie asked, scowling.

She just shrugged, and Mr. Malloy said, "Have fries, Ben."

"But I want onion rings."

"Well, they don't have them, Benjie," Mrs. Malloy said brightly, but her voice sounded strained.

Mitzi expected her brother to put up a fuss, but for some reason he just shrugged after a moment and muttered, "Fine, I'll have the stupid fries."

After the waitress had finished taking their orders and walked away, Benjie said, "How come this place had to change the jukebox *and* the menu?"

"Everything changes, Ben," Mr. Malloy said, patting his shoulder.

"It was really good the way it was."

Mrs. Malloy stood up. "Excuse me," she said, "I'm going to the ladies' room."

She hurried away, and she was gone for a really long time. When she came back, Mitzi thought her face seemed different—like she had taken off some of her eye makeup or something.

The knot in her stomach tightened, and when her chili and potato skins came, she felt like she didn't even want them. But she ate them anyway, and she made her own jukebox selections—an old song by Ace of Base, for herself, and a *really* old one by Michael Bolton, for her parents. She didn't particularly like the song, but she remembered that her parents had slow-danced to it at her Aunt Lisa's wedding reception last year, acting all romantic and whispering to each other on the dance floor.

She looked at them now when the song came on, to see if it seemed to have triggered any memories. But her mother was wiping ketchup off Max's face and her father was pushing his plate away. She noticed that he hadn't finished his steak or his baked potato.

"Everyone done eating?" he asked, looking around the table.

Benjie, of course, was long-finished—he always gobbled everything in, like, two bites. Mitzi had polished off her chili and most of her potato skins, and even Max had done a good job on his burger. But their mother's plate was still full—in fact, her chicken stir-fry looked untouched.

For some reason, Mitzi's father didn't seem to notice. He just cleared his throat, looked at his wife, and then around the table at all of them.

"Can I choose my songs now?" Max asked.

"Uh, one second there, okay, Max?" Mr. Malloy said. "Your mom and I want to talk to you guys about something."

Mitzi's stomach did a sickening flip-flop. She looked from her mother to her father.

Suddenly, she wondered why she had thought things were back to normal just a little while ago.

Nothing seemed normal.

Her father was acting all stiff and strange. Her mother looked like she'd been crying or something. And even Captain Bob's didn't have strawberry milkshakes on the menu anymore.

"Hi, Mitz? It's me."

"Oh, hi, Nikki," she said into the phone.

"You were supposed to stop over and say goodbye after dinner, remember?"

"I know, but . . ." Mitzi twisted the phone cord around her pinky, cutting off the circulation so that the tip turned an angry red. "We went to Captain Bob's, and by the time we got home, it was too late . . . you know, my parents don't like me outside after dark and stuff."

There was a pause. "Right. Well, I just wanted to see you before I leave tomorrow morning, but I guess I won't."

"I guess not." Mitzi wrapped more of the phone cord around the rest of her finger so that you couldn't see any skin, just a tube of rubbery-plastic rings.

"Mitzi?"

"Yeah?"

"Is everything all right? I mean, are you mad at me for going away to camp and leaving you behind?"

"Uh-uh. Why would I be mad?"

"I don't know. You just sound funny. And when your mom called you to the phone I thought I heard you say for her to tell me you weren't home."

"Oh." That was exactly what she'd said. She had been lying on her bed staring at the ceiling when her mother had called up the stairs that Nikki was on the phone. But either her mother hadn't heard what she'd said, or she'd ignored her. "I didn't say that," she told Nikki now. "I mean, why would I say that?"

"I don't know. I thought I heard it, that's all."

"Well, you didn't."

"Okay, whatever. So . . . I guess I'll see you in August, right?"

"I guess so . . ."

"I mean, unless you can come and visit me in Connecticut or something," Nikki added.

"I doubt it," Mitzi told her dully. "But you never know."

"Right. Well, see you, Mitz. Have a good summer."

"Yeah, you too. 'Bye." She hung up the phone and went straight back to her room, slamming the door behind her.

She flopped back on her bed.

Have a good summer.

Yeah.

Right.

How was she supposed to have a good summer when her father was moving out so that her parents could have what they called a "trial separation"?

They just couldn't live together anymore. That was what they'd said in Captain Bob's. Rather, that was what Mitzi's father had said. Mitzi's mother hadn't said much of anything; she'd mostly sat there with tears running down her face, and she kept wiping away at them so that no one else in the restaurant would notice.

No one seemed to. The booths were pretty private, which was obviously why her parents had wanted to sit in one tonight.

And the whole time her father had talked about how this move was the best thing for everyone, and how he would have lots of "quality time" with Mitzi and her brothers, Mitzi had thought that if they were at home and he were saying these things, she would have escaped to her room right away.

But since they were in Captain Bob's, she was trapped, which was probably the whole point of why her parents had chosen to drop their bomb-shell in a public place. After all, Mitzi and her brothers could hardly run crying through the restaurant in front of half the town of Somerset.

No, they'd been forced to sit there and listen to the whole speech, during which Mitzi had rolled and unrolled the corner of her paper place mat, and Benjie had scowled at everyone and everything, and Max, who didn't really get it, had kept interrupting to ask if he could choose his jukebox songs.

Mitzi had managed to keep from crying the whole way home. Even after she had gotten to her room and was lying on her bed, the tears wouldn't come. What she felt instead was anger.

Why were her parents being so stupid?

Didn't they know that they weren't the kind of family who did things like this? They were supposed to be a normal family, like Nikki's, with two parents living together under one roof. Her father wasn't supposed to go off and live in some stupid apartment, like Rascal Timmons's father did.

A horrible thought struck Mitzi as she flopped down on her bed again after hanging up with Nikki.

What if her father started going out on dates, like Mr. Timmons did? What if her mother got married again, to some creep, like Rascal's mother had? What if she decided to have more kids with her new husband? Rascal had two bratty little half brothers now.

But Mitzi's parents hadn't said anything about a divorce. Just a separation, she reminded herself.

Which wasn't necessarily a good sign, but it was better than a divorce.

Hopefully, her parents would come to their senses and realize how much they missed each other after a few days apart. Then, hopefully, her father would come back home where he belonged.

But what if he didn't?

What if they really did end up divorced?

Mitzi kept her eyes from blinking for as long as she could, knowing that as soon as she let them close, the tears would start spilling over.

And when they finally did, they kept coming, and she cried for a long, long time, until her head was throbbing and her eyes felt hot and sore.

Then she lay there in the dark, and whispered, "Please don't let this happen. Please. Please make everything be all right again."

She didn't know who she was talking to—her parents, or God, or whoever. But she kept whispering into the dark until she finally drifted off to sleep.

* * *

"She needs me," Maddie said to Justin. "What do I do?"

"That's up to you," he said, shrugging. "You're her guardian angel."

"But up until now, it's been easy, except that one day when she was three and started choking on that grape while she was alone in her crib. That was tricky."

"You got her through that. You'll get her through this."

"This is different. That time, I knew she had the grape in her pocket when she went in for her nap, and all I had to do was wait for her to swallow it. This is way more complicated. And I know exactly how she feels right now," Maddie said, thinking back to the day her own parents had first announced that they were splitting up.

"That's why you're the perfect person to help her."

"But Justin, I have no control over what her mother and father do. I can't get them back together for her."

"No one said you should."

"After all, you didn't get my parents back together for me," she continued.

"Nope," Justin agreed, and shook his head. "That would have been a disaster. They're both much better off now."

"They sure are," Maddie said, smiling.

She allowed herself a quick peek at her mother, who was back home in Silver Falls, just slipping into bed beside her second husband, Thomas, who she had met at a bereaved parents group meeting a year after Maddie's death.

Then she made a swift check on her father, who was snoring peacefully on his gently rocking houseboat in the Florida Keys, where he spent his days fishing and enjoying peace and solitude.

Satisfied that her parents were fine, Maddie drifted back to Mitzi, who was finally asleep on her tear-dampened pillow. Poor thing.

Downstairs, she saw Mitzi's mother, Carol, sitting at the kitchen table in her bathrobe, drinking coffee and brooding. And across town, she saw Mitzi's father, Will, trying to get comfortable on a lumpy mattress in a drafty little apartment above a sheet-music store.

"Come on, Justin, what am I supposed to do now?" Mitzi asked him, shaking her head doubtfully.

"I can't give you the answers, Maddie. This is your big challenge. This is the one that might earn you your wings."

"You said that the last time, when she choked on the grape."

"Well, that turned out to be too easy. All you

had to do was pop in and do the Heimlich maneuver, then pop out again."

"It *was* pretty simple."

"This time, she's calling out to you for help, Maddie. You can't let her down."

"But I'm stumped. How did you help me when my parents split up? You *did* help me get through it . . . didn't you?"

"Of course." Justin gave her a mysterious little smile. "But you know I can't tell you how. You know a human being's memory of an encounter with a guardian angel always fades until . . ."

"I know. Until you get to heaven, and you get all of your memories back." Maddie shook her head and sighed. "If I don't get my act together and figure out how to help poor Mitzi, I'll never get into heaven."

"You will too," Justin said, and patted her arm. "Just give it some thought."

"I will," Maddie said, reaching into the bag of cookies she kept in her pocket at all times. "And somehow, I always think better when I'm chewing."

Chapter Three

It had been two weeks since Mitzi's father had moved out. Two endless, awful weeks. She had spent most of her time lying on her bed, staring at the ceiling, or trying to read or watch TV.

Benjie and Max spent their days at the summer day camp at the Y. Mrs. Malloy dropped them off every day on her way to work and picked them up on her way home.

There were only four of them around the dinner table at night now, and Benjie and Max were always full of chatter about what they'd done all day at camp. You'd think the two of them hadn't even noticed that things were different now—that something was missing. *Someone.* Their own father, for heaven's sake. Didn't they care?

Mitzi knew Max was too young to really understand. But you'd think Benjie would have the decency to be as miserable as she was about their parents' split. You didn't see *her* chattering and laughing and asking for third helpings of everything.

At least, her mother seemed subdued. She didn't eat or talk as much as she used to—or yell as much, either, which Mitzi probably should have seen as a good thing.

Like, the other night, when Mitzi accidentally put a banana peel down the garbage disposal and it turned into a stringy, ropelike mass that clogged the machinery, her mother didn't even freak out. She just shook her head, looking tired, and said, "We'll have to call a repairman to come over and fix it."

"I bet Dad could do it," Mitzi said hopefully. "He always knows how to fix stuff. And that way, you wouldn't have to pay someone."

But her mother had just sighed, shook her head again, and dialed the repairman's number.

"Careful on that bottom step, guys—it's uneven," Mr. Malloy said, opening the door and ushering them into a dark little entryway at the foot of the steep flight that led up to his apartment.

This was their second Sunday together. Last week, they'd spent the whole day visiting Grandma and Grandpa Malloy up in Albany, which had felt kind of normal, except that Mitzi's mom wasn't around.

Today, it was raining, and they'd gone to a matinee at the mall—some dumb action movie Benjie had insisted on seeing. Now here they were, about to see where Mr. Malloy had been living for the past two weeks.

Mitzi followed her father up the stairs. He was carrying a pizza in one hand and was holding Max's hand with his free one. Benjie darted up ahead of everyone and pushed open the door at the top.

"Where's the lights, Dad?" he called.

"There's a switch by the door, on the right. I've got it," Mr. Malloy said, reaching the top step and letting go of Max's hand. He flicked a switch, and light spilled down the steps.

Mitzi, who was trudging slowly, trying to put off arriving at her destination, could see that the walls along the stairs were water-stained and covered with some ugly yellowish wallpaper that looked like it was a million years old.

Why would her father want to live in this horrible place when he could be in their big, comfortable two-story house in a nice neighborhood? This stupid apartment was right on Market Street in downtown Somerset, in an ugly box of a brick building that had a sheet-music store on the first floor and was next door to the only Laundromat in town.

"Come on up, Mitzi," her father said, holding the door open and waiting for her.

She reached the top step and reluctantly entered the apartment. She found herself standing in a small, square living room. There was a worn brown couch, a matching chair, a couple of small tables, and a portable television set on top of a wobbly-looking bookcase. Mitzi couldn't tell if the area rug was gray or green, but it was definitely ugly.

On one of the tables, there was a framed photo of Mitzi and her brothers that her parents had taken at Sears. It was at least two years old, and none of them even looked the same anymore.

"Where did you get that old picture?" Mitzi asked her father, who seemed to be waiting for her to say something about the apartment. She could hear her brothers in the next room. It sounded like they were jumping on a bed or something.

"It was in my office," her father said, looking a little uncomfortable.

"Well, why don't you put a newer one up? Like the family picture the photographer took at Aunt Lisa's wedding?"

He cleared his throat and said, "Good idea," like he didn't mean it. "Come on, Mitzi, let me give you the rest of the tour."

She allowed herself to be led into a tiny, old-fashioned kitchen that had a stained porcelain sink and a narrow stove that was half the size of theirs at home. The cupboards were made of ugly dark wood and the yellow linoleum on the floor was curling up at the edges.

The bedroom was next. Sure enough, Benjie and Max had been jumping on the bed, had collided in midair, and now Benjie had a bloody lip and Max was crying and rubbing his head. Mitzi calmed him down while her father cleaned Benjie's lip in the bathroom, which was off the bedroom.

Mitzi noticed that he didn't tell Benjie that he should have known better than to jump on the bed, which was what he would have said in the good old days. He just listened and nodded while Benjie described the "death-defying" stunt he had been practicing when Max's head had gotten in the way.

Then he said, "Come on, guys, the pizza's probably getting cold."

"We can just put it in the microwave, can't we?" Mitzi asked.

"I don't have one," her father said.

"Oh," she said, and fought back a little twinge of guilt, because she'd known that. She just couldn't understand why he'd want to live here, with this awful, old-fashioned kitchen, instead of back home, where they had a new microwave and a dishwasher and nice, bright glass-front cupboards.

But even though she felt guilty, she couldn't help saying, as they walked toward the kitchen, "I'll set the table."

"There is no table," her father said.

"There's not?" she asked, as if she was surprised. "Then where are we going to eat?"

"In the living room. It'll be fun. Like a picnic."

"The living room? Can we watch TV?" Max asked, brightening.

"Sure we can," Mr. Malloy said.

"Cool," Benjie said, and Max echoed him.

At home, they hadn't been allowed to eat in the living room ever since they got new furniture and carpeting a few years ago. Mrs. Malloy said she didn't want crumbs and spills all over the place.

Well, Mitzi thought, it was a good thing this apartment was so shabby and old. Her father didn't yell when Max dropped his pizza face-down on the couch or when Benjie knocked his full glass of grape juice all over the gray-or-green rug.

But by the time he dropped them off back at home at the end of the night, he looked pretty frazzled. Mitzi realized she couldn't remember the last time her father had spent hours alone with the three of them. Had he ever? And was this what he meant by quality time?

If so, maybe he'd get sick of it really fast and decide he wanted to come back home. That way, he could go back to spending his Sundays doing yard work, reading the paper, and watching the game on TV.

"Aren't you coming in, Dad?" Mitzi asked when he pulled into the driveway.

"Uh-uh," he said, helping Max zip his raincoat.

"How come? Don't you want to say hi to Mom? I mean, you haven't seen her in two weeks," Mitzi pointed out.

"I know . . . tell her hello for me, okay?" her father said, leaning over to ruffle her hair and give her a kiss goodbye.

"Fine," Mitzi said shortly, opening her car door and stepping out into the gloomy rainy night.

As she splashed her way to the door, with her brothers lagging along behind her to jump into puddles and squish through the mud, she decided she had never felt more alone or miserable in her entire life.

"Maddie, do you mean to tell me that you still haven't come up with a plan?"

She shook her head reluctantly and bit into a chocolate macadamia nut crunch cookie. "I'm still thinking—see?" she told Justin as she chewed furiously and scrunched up her eyes as if deep in thought. "Really. I just don't know what to do yet."

"Well, you'd better come up with something fast," he said, pointing at poor Mitzi, who was sopping wet from head to toe and crying as she wrung her clothes out up in her room. "Look at her. She needs you, Maddie."

"I *know* she does, Justin," she said worriedly, and reached into her bag for another cookie, this one a macaroon with a dollop of fudge on top. "And I'm going to help her. You'll see. I just need to figure out *how*."

Monday morning was one of those beautiful days that follow rainy nights. Mitzi looked out her bedroom window and saw that the world seemed to have been washed clean, and now everything sparkled under cloudless blue skies and the sun's golden glow.

It would be a good idea to get out of the house today. Mitzi couldn't stand the thought of spending another second cooped up in her room feeling sorry for herself.

She took a shower and got dressed, then ate breakfast and went around the house finding all her library books, which were due tomorrow anyway. Then she put them into her backpack and set out on the twenty-minute walk down-town.

As she walked, she thought about her parents and wondered how she could get them back together again. It wasn't going to be easy, considering that they didn't even want to *see* each other. If only she could throw them together somehow . . .

And then, out of nowhere, the idea struck her.

It was perfect.

It was foolproof.

All she had to do was run away.

If she disappeared for a few days, her parents would panic. They would have to get together to look for her, right? And if they got together and focused on something other than fighting for a change, they would remember how much they loved each other.

There was only one problem.

Where would she go?

To her grandparents' house in Albany?

Nah. Even if she explained her great plan, they'd tell her parents where she was in about two seconds.

To visit Nikki at horse camp in Connecticut?

Nah. The counselors would probably notice an extra girl hanging around for a few days, and besides, the only horses she'd ever ridden were plastic and attached to the merry-go-round at the county fair.

Mitzi kept walking, trying to come up with another idea, but she kept drawing blanks.

Her mother's sister, Aunt Lisa, and her husband, Uncle Josh, were pretty cool. But even if Mitzi could count on them not to tell her parents where she was, they lived right here in town, and Mitzi's mother was always dropping by their condo to have coffee.

Her mother's parents, Grandma and Grandpa Hayden, lived *too* far away—down in Florida, near their youngest daughter, Aunt Patty.

Her father's sister, Aunt Val, lived overseas in Germany, where she was in the army. So she, too, was out of the question.

Well, who said Mitzi had to stay with someone?

In fact, it would be better if she didn't get anyone else involved in her plan. That way, there was less chance of running into a problem.

Mitzi quickened her steps as she headed toward the library, her feet keeping pace with her racing mind.

All she had to do was come up with a place where no one would notice a twelve-year-old girl hanging around alone for a few days.

Bingo!

New York City.

Mitzi knew, from class trips, that it was less than two hours away from Somerset by bus. She also knew that it was enormous and that everyone there rushed around, too busy to notice what anyone else was doing.

Okay, so she had her plan. She'd run away to New York City for a few days, just long enough for her parents to get back together.

Now there was only one last problem to work out.

Money.

She needed bus fare to the city. And she needed to buy food while she was there, too, although she could probably eat at McDonald's most of the time. And she needed money for a motel while she was there—no way was she going to sleep outside in some park. She hated bugs, and everyone knew New York City was full of bugs.

How much would a motel room cost? The Somerset Motor Inn had a sign out front that said ROOMS—$39.99/NIGHT, but everyone knew things were more expensive in the city. A room there could be as much as fifty dollars a night— maybe even *sixty*.

Where was she going to get that kind of money?

A job!

That was where.

She'd just have to get a job, she thought, turning the corner in front of the Somerset Public Library and walking briskly toward the wide stone steps.

And she knew just where to look. There was a bulletin board in the lobby of the library where people put up notices advertising things they wanted to sell, or services they offered or needed.

Excited, she practically ran up the steps to the heavy double glass doors.

"Uh-oh," Maddie said, wringing her hands. "I can't let her do this."

Justin nodded. "That's for sure. A twelve-year-old girl can't go to New York City alone. Do you realize how dangerous that is? And Mitzi is pretty sheltered and naive. She wouldn't last ten minutes in the Port Authority Bus Terminal, Maddie."

"I *know* that, Justin. I have to stop her."

"Well, you'd better put a move on it. Once she gets a job and starts saving her money, it's only a matter of time before she takes off."

"I know, I know, but . . ." Maddie chewed on her bottom lip for a moment, then slapped herself on the head and shouted gleefully, "I've got it!"

Chapter Four

Mitzi ran most of the way home from the library, stopping only when she absolutely had to, to catch her breath. Her empty knapsack bounced along on her back—she hadn't bothered to choose new books. There hadn't been time. Not after she found what she found.

It had been the strangest thing . . .

As soon as she'd walked in the front door of the library, she'd scanned the bulletin board in the lobby, checking the thumbtacked notices for anything that said Help Wanted and could apply to her. People had put up flyers to sell pianos and computers and to announce that they were available to provide child care in their homes and to announce bake sales and car washes.

There were a few Help Wanted flyers, too, but nothing suitable for a twelve-year-old girl, except maybe the one that wanted someone to mow a lawn and clip hedges every Saturday. Mitzi thought she could do that, but then she saw the last line, which said "candidates must have own rider lawnmower and hedge clippers." Even if she could borrow her father's lawnmower, it wasn't a rider, and she knew he didn't have hedge clippers because there weren't any hedges around their house—only flowers and trees.

Discouraged, Mitzi had walked away from the bulletin board, but then suddenly, something had made her go back. And as she stood there scanning it one last time, she realized that she'd missed something.

Something important.

And she didn't know *how* she could have missed it because the flyer was fluorescent pink and printed in bold black block letters.

HELP WANTED IMMEDIATELY:

LOCAL GIRL
NEEDED FOR LIGHT HOUSEHOLD WORK
MUST BE RESPONSIBLE AND DEDICATED
AVAILABLE WEEKDAYS
11–13 YEARS OLD

GREAT PAY!

CALL 555-4256

Mitzi had been so excited she'd ripped the flyer off the bulletin board and run out of the library, pausing out front only to dump her books into the night-deposit bin.

Now, as she hurried up the front steps of her house, she still clutched the bright pink paper in her hand. Luckily, no one was home. She went straight to the telephone and quickly dialed the number, then cleared her throat and took a deep breath.

"Hello?" A musical female voice answered on the first ring.

"Hi. My name is Mitzi Malloy, and I saw your help-wanted flyer at the library?"

"Yes?"

"And I'm calling because I know I'm the perfect person for the job," she said in a rush. "I'm great at light household work—heavy household work, too, and I'm responsible and dedicated and available weekdays . . . and I'm twelve."

"You're right," the voice said. "You are perfect for the job. You're hired."

Mitzi nearly dropped the receiver. "I'm sorry . . . did you say I'm *hired?*"

"Yup."

For a moment, she was so startled she couldn't speak. She couldn't believe landing a job could be this easy. Didn't the woman want to meet her? Or call references? Or . . . something?

But why would she? Mitzi's inner voice protested. *You just told her everything she needs to know.*

"Er . . . when do you want me to start?" she asked, trying not to sound too eager but unable to think of anything to say instead.

The answer was a decisive, "Tomorrow at ten. Do you know where Grimby Manor is?"

"Uh-huh." Everyone in Somerset knew that exclusive street, but only a handful of wealthy people actually lived on it.

"It's the last house on the left–number twenty-one, just before the dead end. There's a black iron fence around the place. You can't miss it. The gate will be open for you, so come on up to the front door."

"Okay," Mitzi agreed, her mind whirling. There were so many other questions she needed to ask, but . . . what were they? She was still too stunned at having landed a job so quickly to be able to think clearly.

"See you tomorrow, then," the voice said, and before Mitzi could stop her, the person had hung up with a lilting, "Goodbye."

Wait! Mitzi thought frantically.

She didn't know the person's name, or how much she was going to get paid, or exactly what kind of work she was going to be doing.

But then, did any of that really matter?

She had a job!

Her plan was in motion.

In no time at all, she'd have money in her pocket and a bus ticket for New York City in her hand.

And soon after that, she'd have a normal family again.

"Well?" Maddie asked Justin triumphantly. "What do you think?"

"I think you're crazy," he said flatly. "You've gone and given her the one thing she shouldn't have—a job. The point was to keep her from making money so you could keep her at home—remember? And how is this helping her, emotionally? She's still torn apart over her parents' separation."

"Trust me, Justin," Maddie said confidently, biting into a sugar cookie shaped like a star. "I know exactly what I'm doing."

He shook his head. "I certainly hope so."

"What did you think of that phone number I conjured up?"

"What about it?"

"555-4256. Don't you get it?"

"Get what?"

Maddie snapped her fingers and produced a cordless telephone. "Look at the keypad. 555-4256 is 555-H-A-L-O. Halo! Get it?"

"Clever."

"Don't roll your eyes at me like that, Justin," she said, popping the last of her star cookie into her mouth. "Mitzi Malloy is in good hands now. Just wait and see."

Chapter Five

Grimby Manor was a ten-minute bike ride from Mitzi's house on Rebecca Court, but she had allowed herself a half hour, just in case. She didn't want to be late on her first day at her new job.

She hadn't told her parents about it. Her father wasn't around anyway, and her mother worked on weekdays. If she asked Mitzi what she'd been doing with her days, she could just make something up.

She rode slowly down the wide, tree-lined lane, noticing the difference between this neighborhood and her own. Here, the yards were large and lush and manicured, and the houses were set far apart from each other and way back from the road. There were no basketball hoops over these garages; no tricycles or wagons or jump ropes carelessly left on these lawns. You couldn't smell bacon frying or hear dogs barking or kids shouting to each other.

In fact, by the time she got to the end of the street, Mitzi hadn't seen a single other person or heard any sound except lawn sprinklers spraying. As she hopped off her bike she decided it was almost eerie.

She walked toward the tall iron fence marked with a gold-toned "21," and felt a flicker of hesitation . . .

But it vanished the moment she caught a glimpse of what was beyond the fence.

The grounds looked like paradise, all green and woodsy, with beautiful flowers blooming in gardens and on bushes and trees. The house itself was like a gingerbread confection, painted a dozen shades of pink, with scalloped shingles and curlicue trim and graceful peaks and cozy nooks and crannies.

The gate in the center of the fence was ajar, and Mitzi swiftly wheeled her bike through. She parked it off to the side of the winding white gravel driveway, which actually seemed to sparkle in the sun, almost as though the stones were made partly of diamonds.

"Here goes," she whispered to herself and walked the dozen or so yards up the driveway to the front porch. She climbed the steps, rang the old-fashioned round doorbell, and waited, crossing her fingers inside her shorts pocket for good luck.

The door was thrown open almost instantly, as though someone had been waiting just on the other side.

Mitzi didn't know what—or who—she had been expecting, but it wasn't this teenaged girl who stood there, smiling.

"Hi. You must be Mitzi," she said, and Mitzi noticed that her voice had a familiar musical quality.

"I am. Are you . . . the person I talked to on the phone yesterday?" she asked doubtfully. She'd been under the impression that the person who'd hired her had been an adult, but . . .

"No," the girl said breezily. "That was my mom. She couldn't be here right now, so she asked me to get you started. I'm Madeline."

Mitzi nodded politely.

"But call me Maddie," the girl added, tossing her chestnut-colored hair, which was caught back in a filmy white scarf, headband-style. She had a round, rosy-cheeked face and warm, wide, sky-blue eyes. She wasn't much taller than Mitzi and seemed slender, though it was hard to tell because she wore a loose-fitting white T-shirt over baggy white shorts. The white sneakers on her feet were so spotless that Mitzi guessed they'd never been worn before.

Suddenly, she was conscious of her own

scuffed Nikes, frayed denim shorts, and old navy polo shirt with the bleach stain by the hem in the back. She'd dressed as she would if she were going to help her mother clean, but now she wondered if she should have dressed up a little. After all, this place seemed so . . . upscale.

"Come on in," Maddie said, stepping back and motioning her into the high-ceilinged entrance hall. A wide, curving staircase led up to a second-floor balcony that was lined with closed doors.

Through an archway that led off to the right, Mitzi could see a large living room with lots of plush-looking furniture, a grand piano, a fireplace, and floor-to-ceiling windows.

"This way," Maddie said, leading her straight ahead and down a long hallway. They ended up in an enormous, sparkling kitchen with gleaming appliances and miles of counters.

"Have a seat," Maddie offered, pointing at the table in a sunny nook. "We'll get to know each other. Want some milk and cookies?"

"Milk and cookies?" Mitzi hesitated. She was supposed to be starting her new job, wasn't she? Not having snacks and chatting. What if Maddie's mother came home and decided she was lazy or something and fired her?

"It's fine," Maddie said, as though she'd read her mind. "Mom won't mind."

"Okay." Mitzi sat down. She *was* kind of starving.

Within moments, a tall, cold glass of milk was in front of her, along with a plate piled high with different kinds of cookies.

"Help yourself," Maddie said, carefully choosing three for herself—a gingerbread man, a frosted chocolate one, and a sugar-topped molasses one.

Mitzi took what looked like oatmeal and raisin and bit in. Mmm . . . it was the best cookie she'd ever tasted.

"Great, huh?" Maddie said with her mouth full. "I love cookies, don't you? I love baking them and everything."

"Yup. Did you . . . make all these yourself?"

Maddie's eyes twinkled. "I had a little help."

"Your mom?"

"No, she's . . . she works a lot."

Mitzi nodded. "Mine does, too."

"What does she do?"

"She works in the billing office at the hospital."

"How about your dad?"

"He's in insurance."

"Are they divorced?" Maddie asked, and Mitzi almost choked on her cookie.

"No . . . why?" she asked when she could speak.

Maddie shrugged. "Mine are. A lot of people are."

"Well, my parents aren't," Mitzi said firmly. Then something made her add, "Yet."

"Separated?"

"How did you know?"

"Lucky guess," Maddie said. "Look, I know how you feel right now. It stinks when your dad moves out. Is yours still here in town?"

"Yes, but—"

"When my dad left, he went to Florida to live on a boat and fish. It was what he'd always wanted to do, but he got married to my mom and had me instead."

Mitzi didn't know what to say to that. It had never occurred to her that her father could leave town. What if her parents did end up divorced, and he left?

"But," Maddie added with a shrug, "things are fine now. He's really happy, and so is Mom. And so am I."

Yeah, right, Mitzi thought. No one could possibly be happy when their family was ripped apart that way.

She stood up abruptly. "I'd better get to work now."

"Don't you want another cookie?"

"No, thanks."

"Well, okay . . ." Maddie, who had finished all three of hers, grabbed a chocolate chip one and said, "Come on—I'll show you what you're supposed to do."

Work, Mitzi decided as she pedalled home that afternoon with a crisp new twenty dollar bill in her pocket, was great.

All she'd had to do was dust all the furniture in the house with a feather duster. Sure, there was a lot of it, and most of it was carved, old-fashioned pieces with lots of little crevices. But there was hardly any dust anywhere, so it wasn't exactly a chore.

She'd had a lunch break outside on a blanket under a tree with Maddie, who had made peanut butter and jelly sandwiches and delicious icy lemonade. They'd talked a lot, but luckily, Maddie didn't bring up the subject of her parents or Mitzi's again. Mitzi didn't want to talk about it, especially with a stranger . . . although Maddie didn't really seem like a stranger. She was so easygoing and talkative that Mitzi felt as though she were an old friend by the end of the day.

To her surprise, Maddie's mother never did come home, and it was Maddie who paid her when she'd finished dusting.

"See you tomorrow at ten," she'd said, and Mitzi had smiled and nodded, realizing she was looking forward to it.

Now, as she turned the corner onto Rebecca Court and saw her house up ahead, she reminded herself that she was working for a reason—to save enough money to put her plan into action so she could save her parents' marriage.

But that didn't mean she couldn't enjoy it—or that she couldn't make a new friend while she was at it.

"All you have to do today," Maddie said, "is help with the baking."

"The baking?" Mitzi noticed that she found herself repeating a lot of things Maddie said. That was because Maddie kept surprising her.

Like, yesterday when she'd arrived at work, Maddie had said that they were going to be working together, alphabetizing all the books in the study, and that Mitzi could borrow any she liked. To Mitzi's amazement, the shelves had contained all of her favorite series. Maddie had read them all, and when Mitzi left that afternoon, she was balancing a bagful of books on her handlebars.

Today, it seemed, she and Maddie were going to bake cookies together in the big, homey kitchen. Outside there was a summer storm— rain and wind and thunder and lightning.

"Isn't it the perfect day for this?" Maddie

asked happily, pulling down ingredients from the cupboards.

Mitzi agreed that it was, and lined everything up on the counter: flour and sugar—granulated, confectioners', and brown—baking powder and baking soda; chocolate, butterscotch, and peanut butter chips; coconut and maraschino cherries and nuts and sprinkles.

"What kind of cookies are we making?" she asked Maddie.

"Every kind we can think of."

"Won't your mom mind if we use all this stuff up?"

"Nah."

Mitzi wondered, not for the first time, about Maddie's mother. She had yet to meet her. And, she realized, she had no idea what she even looked like—there weren't any pictures of her around the house.

Which seemed odd, actually.

Mitzi thought of her own house, where photos and snapshots were in frames on tables and walls and were even pinned to the refrigerator with magnets. And since her parents subscribed to practically every magazine that existed, there were stacks of them in every room, along with a clutter of bills and newspaper clippings and stuff like that.

Maddie's house, in sharp contrast, had few

personal touches. Oh, it was cozy and homey and everything, but Mitzi had dusted the whole place from top to bottom, and she hadn't noticed any personal items around. It was kind of like the furnished condo her family had rented in Florida last spring. Generic and almost too perfect.

"Mitzi? Can you get the butter and eggs and milk out of the fridge?" Maddie asked, breaking into her thoughts.

"Oh . . . sure," she said, moving slowly to the refrigerator.

She opened it and started removing the items, noticing as she did that they were all in sealed containers. And the other stuff on the shelves looked too perfect—smooth-skinned plums and peaches in a bowl, a full pitcher of lemonade and one of iced tea, whole bottles of condiments, and unopened packages of cheese and cold cuts.

There were no cellophane-covered bowls of leftovers, no foil-wrapped slices of pizza, no sticky half-empty jelly jars.

"Mitzi?" Maddie's voice was right behind her, making her jump. "Is everything all right?"

"Oh . . . yeah, I just sort of blanked out for a second," she said, backing away from the fridge and kicking the door closed with her foot.

"Good thing Mom went shopping last night," Maddie said in her musical voice, taking the milk out of Mitzi's hand and carrying it and a measuring cup over to the counter. "We were out of everything."

Oh, so that was it, Mitzi thought, relieved. For a second there, she had been a little spooked. But that was ridiculous.

After all, Maddie was the most normal person she'd ever met.

But still, Mitzi couldn't help thinking about the absence of photos and other items around the house. And, she realized belatedly, the phone hadn't rung once in the week since she'd been working here.

Not that it meant anything.

But she couldn't help wondering . . .

"Well? What do you think? How am I doing so far?" Maddie asked Justin breathlessly.

He shrugged. "She's happier, and you're certainly keeping her occupied, if that's your mission. But you'd better be careful . . . she's getting a little suspicious. You don't want to scare her off."

"I know, I know . . ." Maddie shook her head. "I figured I'd thought of everything, but I guess I missed a few details. Don't worry, though . . . I'll fix things next week."

"Don't you think she'll notice if there's suddenly, like, a huge family portrait on the wall over the fireplace?''

''Trust me, Justin. I know what I'm doing,'' Maddie assured him with a contented little smile.

Chapter Six

Since everything was closed on Monday to celebrate the Fourth of July, Maddie had told Mitzi to take the day off. She and her brothers spent it with their father up at her grandparents' house in Albany, which was what they always did on the Fourth, except that Mitzi's mother had always been there before.

Mrs. Malloy usually drove everyone crazy with her worrying—she worried when they went swimming in the pond down the road, and when they ate the potato salad after it had been out in the sun, and when Grandpa's neighbor George showed up after supper with his illegal fireworks.

But this year, Mitzi found herself wishing her mother were there to tell her brothers not to go into the deep water when they were at the pond. And when Max got scared when George lit the first Roman candle, she gave her father a look that said, *See what happens when Mom's not around?* But her father didn't seem to notice. He was busy talking to George's grown-up daughter, Lynne.

All in all, it was the worst Fourth of July Mitzi had ever had.

On Tuesday morning, she wasn't in the greatest mood when she arrived at Maddie's to find several boxes in the middle of the entrance hall.

"What's all this?" she asked.

"The rest of our stuff. It just arrived over the weekend," Maddie told her. "That's your job for today . . . to help me put it all where it belongs."

"But what is it?"

"Oh, photo albums and stuff like that. Mom was really worried because when we moved here, these boxes somehow got separated from everything else."

"I didn't know you had just moved here," Mitzi said, feeling a little twinge of relief. That explained a lot of the things that had been bothering her.

"Yeah, we came from Missouri not too long ago," Maddie told her.

Mitzi was about to ask more about it when the phone rang.

"Be right back—you can start unpacking,"

Maddie told her, and hurried into the next room.

As Mitzi bent over the first box, she heard Maddie pick up the phone and say, "Oh, hi, Thea. I was wondering when you were going to call . . ."

While Maddie chatted with what was obviously an old friend, Mitzi started taking items out of the box. The first thing she removed was a photo album. Feeling slightly sneaky but too curious not to peek, she opened it and saw snapshots of a younger Maddie and a pretty brown-haired woman standing in front of Niagara Falls.

Obviously, this was her mother.

Mitzi wondered again when she was ever going to meet her. Maddie's mother left early every morning for work, and didn't come home until suppertime, according to Maddie.

Mitzi flipped through the pages of the photo album and found snapshots of a slightly older Maddie with a balding, smiling man who was obviously her father. There was light blue water and palm trees in the background.

Again, Mitzi was reminded of her own father, and again she wondered, with a pang, what would happen if her parents got a divorce and her father decided he wanted to move away.

Tears filled her eyes and she struggled not to blink and let them overflow.

"Okay, I'll call you in a couple of days," she heard Maddie say in the next room, and then she heard the phone being replaced in its cradle.

Not wanting Maddie to see her sitting here crying like some stupid baby, Mitzi wiped at her eyes and nose and quickly closed the photo album. She bent her head over the box again as Maddie came back into the room.

"Sorry about the interruption. That was my best friend Thea, from Missouri."

"That's nice."

"Yeah. I miss her. Do you have a best friend?"

"Uh huh. But she's away for the summer, at horse camp in Connecticut. I miss her, too." Come to think of it, Nikki had already sent two postcards and a letter since she'd left, and Mitzi hadn't answered any of them. Which didn't make her a very good friend, she realized guilt-ily. She'd been too wrapped up in her own problems to give Nikki much thought.

"Guess that's how it is, you know?" Maddie said wistfully. "It's like, you get older, and you always find yourself missing someone."

"I guess."

"Like my dad, for instance. I really miss him a lot."

Something in Maddie's tone made Mitzi glance up sharply. Her friend's eyes were suspiciously bright.

"When was the last time you saw him?" Mitzi asked.

"It's been awhile." Maddie cleared her throat. "But it's, like, all right. Because I know he's happy where he is, and I'm happy where I am. Of course I wish things could be the way they used to be, but nothing ever stays the same, Mitzi. You can't stay a little kid forever, just like you can't stay with your parents forever. No matter what. And they can't stay with you."

Mitzi nodded. Something had just occurred to her. She realized that there had been a time when both of her parents had lived at home with *their* parents. And now, her father's parents lived up near Albany, and her mother's parents lived way down in Florida, like Maddie's father did.

She wondered if her parents ever missed their own moms and dads. She had never thought about it before—never thought of her parents as someone's kids . . .

"Mitzi? You all right?"

"I'm fine," she assured Maddie, who was watching her with a concerned expression.

"Okay. Come on, let's get busy then."

Mitzi nodded, pushed her troubling thoughts out of her mind, and reached for the open carton again.

* * *

Mitzi had just finished writing a long letter back to Nikki and was getting ready for bed on Thursday night when there was a knock on her door.

She sighed. "Who is it?"

"It's me," her mother's voice said. "Can I come in?"

"Hang on a second." Mitzi finished pulling her nightgown over her head, then picked up the shorts and shirt she'd tossed on the floor only moments before. Her mother was really into making her put her clothes away these days. She was always going on about how she wasn't the maid and it wasn't her job to pick up after everyone and blah, blah, blah.

Mitzi shoved the shorts into a drawer, jamming them in so she could get it closed again, and stuffed the shirt under her pillow.

Then she plopped down on her bed and called, "All right, come in."

The door opened. Mrs. Malloy came into the room, wearing jeans and an old T-shirt Mitzi's father had brought back for her from a business trip. Mitzi took that as a hopeful sign—maybe her mother was wearing it because she missed him.

"What are you doing in here, Mitzi?" her mother asked, looking around the room like she expected to find something that shouldn't be there. She made a little face, as she always did, when her gaze fell on the built-in bookshelves covered in not just books, but knickknacks, framed photos, Mitzi's soda can collection, and a parade of tiny glass animals. Her mother wasn't crazy about clutter.

"What do you mean, what am I doing?" Mitzi asked, feeling irritated and invaded. "I'm going to bed."

"But you've been in here all night, since supper. Every night for the past few weeks, you're up here behind closed doors. Is everything okay?"

You tell me, Mitzi wanted to say. *How can everything be okay when my father—your husband—isn't even living here anymore?*

But she just kept quiet and looked at her mother, waiting for her to say something else.

She didn't have a long wait.

"Mitzi, I'm worried about you," her mother said, sitting on the edge of the bed and resting a hand on Mitzi's bare ankle.

"How come?"

"I know this is hard for you. You know—your dad and me splitting up."

"Splitting up?" Mitzi pulled her ankle out from under her mother's fingers. "I thought you said you were separated."

"We are."

"Then why'd you just say 'splitting up'?"

Her mother shrugged. "I just meant—"

"Never mind." Mitzi folded her arms in front of her in a swift, fierce movement and stared straight ahead.

There was a pause, and then her mother asked with a falsely casual note, "So what have you been doing with your days?"

"What do you mean?"

"I mean, you always look forward to summer vacation. Are you having fun?"

"I guess."

"Doing what?"

"You know . . . the usual. Riding my bike. Going to the library. Reading. Whatever." She shrugged.

"But it must be lonely this year, with Nikki away."

"Kind of."

Her mother found her ankle again and gave it a pat. "You know what I'm going to do, Mitzi?"

"What?"

"I'm going to take a couple of vacation days next week."

Mitzi's stomach did a queasy little *uh-oh* flip. "How come?"

"Because I want to spend some time with you. What do you think? Wouldn't it be fun? Maybe we'll drive over to Woodbury Common and go outlet shopping or something. We can buy you some new clothes for school."

"School doesn't start again for two months."

"Well then, we'll buy you some summer clothes. There are probably some great sales."

"Mmm hmm." Mitzi's mind was racing. What was she going to do? How was she going to go to her job at Maddie's if her mother was hanging around during the day? "But what about Benjie and Max?" she asked hopefully.

"What about them? They're perfectly fine at day camp. It's been too long since we've had some mother-daughter time together."

Whenever her mom went into that giddy mother-daughter mode, Mitzi always wanted to cringe. Now she was beyond cringing. She was panicking.

Her mother, oblivious, chattered on about how she would tell her boss first thing in the morning that she wanted off on Monday and Tuesday, and he'd better not give her a hard time because after all, she had the time coming, and she had been covering for so-and-so while she was away, and on and on and on.

Finally, her mother wore herself out and stood up, yawning. "Well, I'm going to hit the sack now. I'm really tired. Want me to turn off your light for you?"

"No thanks," Mitzi said. "I'll stay up and read."

"Okay, but not too late."

"I know."

"Goodnight, Mitzi." Her mother bent over

and planted a kiss on the top of her head, something she used to do when Mitzi was little, but hadn't done in a long time.

Mrs. Malloy walked out of the room, closed the door, and went down the hall, whistling. That was another thing she hadn't done in ages, Mitzi realized. She could only hit, like, two notes, but she used to go around cheerfully whistling and getting even louder when anyone complained that she was off-key.

When was the last time her mother had whistled? Mitzi wondered now. Probably not in over a year. Not since she and her dad had gotten into the habit of nightly screaming matches that ended in slammed doors and stony silence.

Mitzi got out of bed and went over to her bookshelf. She reached behind some books and pulled out the envelope she'd stashed there.

Then, sitting cross-legged on her bedroom floor, she counted her money.

And sighed.

It wasn't enough. She'd hoped to save up more than two hundred dollars before she started planning her trip to New York. She wasn't even close to that yet.

And tomorrow was Friday, so the most she would have was another twenty dollars.

But it would have to do. She couldn't wait any longer, thanks to her mother.

Unless . . .

What if she told Maddie that she couldn't come to work for a few days? She could say she was sick . . . or that a family emergency had come up.

But lying to Maddie didn't seem fair, after she had been so nice and everything. And somehow, Mitzi didn't think she could bring herself to look Maddie in the eye and tell a lie. There was something about her that was just too . . . honest. Too good. No, Maddie wasn't someone you lied to.

The time had come for Mitzi's plan to be put into action.

She would run away on Sunday night.

She would write Maddie a letter telling her the whole story, and she'd mail it on Saturday so it would arrive on Monday. That way, she wouldn't be telling a lie, and she wouldn't be running off and leaving Maddie and her mom in a lurch with no explanation.

Since she wouldn't have enough money for a motel, she'd have to make do. Maybe she could sleep in the Port Authority Bus Terminal. There must be a bench in there—bus terminals always had benches. And if there wasn't one, she could just sleep on the floor. It was only for a few nights.

Mitzi sighed, stood up, stuffed the envelope back into her hiding place, and crawled into bed.

Then she turned off the light and lay awake in the dark, planning.

"Uh-oh," Maddie said, watching Mitzi.

"Uh-oh is right," Justin told her. "You have to stop her. She can't sleep on the floor in Port Authority! She won't last the night. Look for yourself—the place is crawling with shady characters."

Maddie peeked down into the mammoth bus terminal and nodded. Despite the late hour, Port Authority was teeming with activity. She saw drug dealers and hustlers and pickpockets, all preying on innocent, unsuspecting people who happened to wander into their path.

Then she checked on Mitzi again, sweet, innocent Mitzi, who lay quietly in her safe suburban bedroom with no idea of what was waiting out there for her.

"I've got to stop her," Maddie told Justin. "And I've got to help her accept what's going on with her parents."

"How are you going to do that?"

"I have no idea," she said grimly, too upset even to think about cookies. "What do you think I should do, Justin?"

He threw up his hands and shook his head.

"Even if I knew, I couldn't tell you, Maddie. This is your deal. You know that."

"I know," she said, nodding. "And I'll figure something out. I *have* to. For Mitzi's sake."

Chapter Seven

Maddie took a hot pan of shortbread cookies out of the oven and set them on a trivet on the counter, then continued what she'd been saying.

"... so anyway, I think that there's really no use for math in the long run in real life."

"I sure hope you're right," Mitzi said, popping a chunk of raw dough from the mixing bowl into her mouth. "Because I really stink at fractions and decimals."

"Just wait till algebra," Maddie told her, shaking her head and poking at a just-baked cookie. "Ow! Too hot," she said, pulling her finger away and sticking it into her mouth.

"You're going to Somerset High this fall, right?" Mitzi asked, taking another tiny piece of dough and promising herself that it would be the last one.

"I . . . uh, sure, I am," Maddie said, nodding.

Then she changed the subject, and Mitzi could have sworn she did it deliberately, though why would she want to do that?

"Uh, Mitzi, I was wondering if you could come a little earlier on Monday morning."

"Why?" Mitzi asked absently, wondering why Maddie seemed distracted all of a sudden. She watched as her friend grabbed a hot shortbread cookie off the tray, then winced and dropped it on the counter.

"Still too hot," Maddie commented, as though she hadn't just figured that out a second ago. "Anyway, because Mom has a major job she needs us to do, and it'll take the whole day. She said to tell you she'll pay you double."

"Double?"

But Monday, she wasn't planning on being around at all. Monday, she would be in New York, and her parents would be frantic with worry . . . and falling in love with each other again.

"This project is *really* important to Mom," Maddie said. "It's something that I can't possibly do alone, so . . ."

"What is it?"

"It's . . . we have to wash all the windows, inside and out."

"Okay." Mitzi nodded guiltily, trying to shut out the image of Maddie struggling to do such a big job on her own. "But isn't there any way we can wait until later next week to do it?"

"Why?"

"Because it's . . . supposed to rain on Monday." She was thinking that after she came back from New York, maybe she could still work for Maddie and her mom, if they still wanted her. After all, she wouldn't mind having some spending money, and she was getting used to hanging around with Maddie.

"Well, it's really a two-day job," Maddie said, "So we can start with the insides on Monday and do the outsides on Tuesday."

"Okay."

Mitzi chewed her lower lip and stared down at the crumbly contents of the mixing bowl. She wanted, more than anything, to come clean with Maddie, to tell her not just that she wouldn't be around on Monday, but why. She had a feeling that Maddie would understand. That Maddie might even be able to help somehow.

But something made her hold back, even though she sensed that Maddie was waiting expectantly, almost as if she knew Mitzi was on the verge of confiding in her.

Finally, she looked up and met Maddie's gaze. "You want me to get a cooling rack for those cookies?"

Was that a flicker of disappointment she saw on her friend's face? Apparently not, because

Maddie just smiled and said, "Sure, there's one in the cupboard to the right of the stove."

And for the rest of the day, Mitzi alternately kicked herself for not spilling the beans, and congratulated herself for keeping her mouth shut.

When Maddie handed over her money at the end of the day, she said, "So I'll see you on Monday morning, a half-hour earlier?"

Mitzi hesitated only a split second before nodding. "Sure," she said brightly. "I'll be here."

Then she got on her bike and rode toward home, wondering why she felt so miserable just when her life was about to fall into place again.

At least, she hoped it was.

It wasn't until Saturday morning that Mitzi realized she didn't know Maddie's last name.

As soon as she got up, she had written a note explaining why she wouldn't be at work on Monday morning. She told the truth—or, most of it, anyway. She said that she was going away to New York City to work out some family problems, and that she hoped Maddie would understand.

Then she pulled an envelope out of her cluttered desk drawer, picked up the pen again to address it . . . and froze. How could she not know Maddie's last name after all this time?

There had to be a way to find out . . .

But if there was, she couldn't think of it.

While she was sitting at her desk, frowning and chewing the blue plastic tip of her pen and wondering, Benjie barged into her room without knocking, as usual.

"Hey!" Mitzi said, scowling at him and hurriedly hiding the letter under her blotter. "What the heck are you doing?"

"We're going to Frolic Island!" Benjie announced, wide-eyed. "Mom said to hurry up and get ready."

Frolic Island? That was the amusement park they had always gone to when they were younger. Mitzi's dad loved the rides, and . . .

Wait a second. Maybe . . .

"Who's going?" Mitzi asked Benjie hopefully.

"Me, you, Mom, and Max . . ."

Her hopes were dashed. No Dad.

". . . and Rascal, if his mom says yes."

This was worse than horrible. A day at Frolic Island without her father, and *with* that dweeb Rascal Timmons.

"Tell Mom I'm not going," Mitzi said, turning back to her desk.

"She said you have to. She said it's family day."

Mitzi turned angrily on Benjie. "It's not exactly family day if the head of the family is missing, is it?"

He shrugged.

Mitzi found herself furious with her brother, for being so caught up in his stupid day camp and in the idea of going to Frolic Island that he didn't seem to care that their dad wasn't around anymore.

Furious with her mother, who seemed to think that she could make everything better by taking them to some amusement park.

Furious with her father, who would rather live alone in some dumpy apartment downtown than with them, at home, where he belonged.

To her horror, she found herself crying.

Crying in front of Benjie, which was something she tried not to do, because he never let her live it down.

She dropped her pen on her desk and buried her face in her hands miserably.

"Geez, Mitzi . . . what's wrong?"

To her surprise, her brother was standing over her, sounding concerned. After a second, she felt his hand on her shoulder, awkwardly patting.

It was so unlike him that she found herself crying harder.

"What?" he asked, starting to sound alarmed.

"Everything's so different," she managed to

get out amidst her tears. "Everything's changing."

She looked up at Benjie and he shrugged, looking at her with ten-year-old wisdom. "I know," he said matter-of-factly. "That's how it is, you know?"

"I guess." She sniffled and looked at her brother affectionately for what was probably the first time since he was, like, a newborn in a bassinet. "Thanks, Ben."

He actually squirmed.

Then his hand darted out and he grabbed the corner of her letter that was sticking out from under the blotter. "What's this?"

"Give me that!" she shrieked, reaching for it.

He scampered toward the door, unfolding it as he went.

Mitzi caught him by the leg just as he lurched toward the hallway, making him tumble to the ground with her on top of him. She managed to get her letter back, but not before it had ripped in half and Ben had asked, "Who the heck is Maddie?"

"None of your business, brat," Mitzi said, getting to her feet and storming back to her room. She slammed the door behind her and stared at the two jagged pieces of paper in her hand.

Now what? Should she rewrite it?

But even if she did, how was she going to

send it? She still didn't know Maddie's last name.

She was still trying to figure out what to do when her mother knocked on her door.

"Mitzi? Are you almost ready?"

"I'm not going," she called back, rolling her eyes.

"Oh, yes you are," her mother said firmly, opening the door a crack and peering into the room. "And we're leaving in ten minutes, so you'd better get a move on."

"But I don't want to go. I hate Frolic Island."

"You've always *loved* Frolic Island, Mitzi," her mother said, sounding tired.

"That's because Dad made it fun."

She knew it was mean of her, and she didn't have to turn around to know that there was a hurt look on her mother's face.

But to her surprise, her mother simply said, after a moment, "Well, since he's not going with us, I guess you'll have to count on me to make it fun, won't you?"

Mitzi didn't reply. She just sat there at her desk, her back to the door.

"Ten minutes, Mitzi. I mean it," her mother said, and she heard the door click closed and footsteps retreating down the hall.

She sat there sullenly for nine minutes, not moving.

Then she spent the last minute frantically digging in her closet for her old Nikes, in case Frolic Island was muddy from all the rain last night.

She put them on hurriedly and ran down the stairs, pretending not to notice her mother's pleased, relieved expression when she showed up in the driveway.

"No, Mitzi, don't do it!" Maddie called out, wincing and covering her eyes with her hands to block out the image of Mitzi at Frolic Island. "Justin, check on her. Is she getting on the Whirling Twirl-a-Curl?"

"Let's see . . . she's stopping to look at it . . . she's tilting her head, thinking about it . . ."

"No, Mitzi!" Maddie repeated, her eyes squeezed shut behind her hands. "I can't look."

"Relax, Maddie," Justin said in his always-calm voice. "Even if she does get on the ride, you know it's probably perfectly safe. They've probably made dozens of improvements since your unfortunate . . . accident."

"Well, I can't let her take any chances," Maddie said. "Be right back."

Justin sighed and nodded.

A few moments later, Maddie popped back in, grinning broadly. "Well? What do you think?"

"Pretty good," Justin admitted, patting her on the back. "Although a few weathermen might wonder where the freak thunderstorm came from when the forecast called for nothing but sunshine from now until next week."

"Don't worry . . . it's only raining in one tiny spot, at Frolic Island. And it's only going to keep up long enough for Mitzi to forget about that stupid ride. Look, now she's perfectly safe, playing skee ball in the arcade."

"Yeah . . . and now that she stopped that kid Rascal from cheating, she's even winning."

Maddie nodded contentedly and reached for her bag of cookies. "I sure am getting the hang of this guardian angel stuff, Justin."

"I wouldn't gloat if I were you. Your biggest challenge is coming up, Maddie. Unless you figure out a way to stop her, Mitzi's going to be on a bus to New York City tomorrow night. And a little rain isn't going to bail her out when she gets into trouble there."

"Don't remind me." Maddie shuddered, thinking about the seedy Port Authority.

"And on top of that," Justin continued, "she's an emotional mess. She still hasn't accepted that her parents might split up. She's still broken-hearted over this whole thing, Maddie. She needs help."

"I know," Maddie said, biting glumly into a gingersnap and shaking her head.

Chapter Eight

On Sunday morning, Mitzi got up early and packed her nylon duffle bag with everything she thought she'd need for her trip. After throwing in several pairs of underwear, socks, shorts, jeans, T-shirts, a sweat shirt, and a spare pair of Nikes, there wasn't much room for anything else.

Still, she managed to squeeze in a zippered floral cosmetics bag containing her toothbrush, toothpaste, Noxema, Clearasil, Secret, and a few hair scrunchies.

Then she crammed in two paperback horror novels, her Walkman and a few cassettes, the new issue of *Sassy*, three packs of gum, and a small umbrella because you never knew when you were going to get caught in a sudden thunderstorm.

She finished packing just as she heard her father's car pull into the driveway to pick them up for their usual Sunday outing.

Mitzi hurriedly forced the zipper closed on her duffel bag. It was so strained at the seams that it looked like it was going to burst open any second. And heavy, too, she realized as she lifted it and searched for a place to stash it until later, just in case her mother decided to snoop while she was gone. Not that snooping was something Mrs. Malloy had ever done before, or was likely to start doing now, but Mitzi wasn't taking any chances.

She tried to stick the bag under her bed, but it wouldn't fit, so she lugged it over to her closet and buried it under the clutter of shoes and boots on the floor there, then covered the whole heap with her bathrobe for good measure.

"Mitzi?"

Was that her father calling her from the foot of the stairs? He hadn't been inside the house since that Friday night when he'd moved out a few weeks ago. Usually, he just honked for them in the driveway.

"Coming!" Mitzi called, closing her closet door. She grabbed her sunglasses and closed the door to her room, then dashed down the stairs.

Sure enough, there was her dad, leaning in the doorway of the living room. He looked tanned and relaxed in his familiar Sunday outfit of baggy blue shorts and a polo shirt.

And he was talking to Mitzi's mother, who was perched on the arm of the couch, and now they were *laughing* about something!

She was so surprised that she paused at the foot of the steps and stared. How long had it been since she had heard her parents carry on a normal conversation, one that wasn't laced with sarcasm and cut-downs and didn't mount rapidly into a screaming match? How long had it been since they had smiled at each other, let alone laughed?

"There you are," Mitzi's dad said, turning and spotting her. "You all set?"

"Uh huh." She walked over and he gave her a hug, as he always did. "What are we doing today?"

"There's a food festival over in Ridge Hills . . . you hungry?" her dad asked, ruffling her hair.

"Sure."

"Okay, then, let's go. Max and Benjie are already outside, waiting. I promised them fried bread dough and cotton candy as soon as we get there."

"Oh, great." Mitzi looked at her mother hopefully. "Are you coming with us, Mom?"

"Am I . . . ? No," her mother said, looking suddenly uncomfortable.

"Why not?" Mitzi asked, as though it were the most normal thing in the world for her mother to be joining them. Not so long ago, it would have been, she reminded herself.

"Your mother has things to do, Mitzi," her father said firmly,

At the same time, her mother said, "I have to meet Aunt Lisa in a half hour."

"Oh." Mitzi shrugged, slipped out from under her father's arm, and headed for the door.

Behind her, she heard him clear his throat and say, "Okay, Carol, I'll have them back by seven-thirty at the latest. Have a good day."

"You, too, Will," her mother said, sounding stiff and formal all of a sudden, just as Mitzi's father did.

The good feelings between them had obviously somehow evaporated, and so did Mitzi's fleeting hope that they might get back together so she wouldn't have to run away tonight.

No, the plan was back on. Tonight at nine-thirty, she would sneak out of the house and catch the late bus to New York City.

She didn't have a choice.

Ridge Hills was a small village on the Hudson River, about ten miles from Somerset. The food festival—a series of booths, each with a different mouth-watering offering—was set up in a park in the center of town. It was jammed.

"Guess everyone had the same idea today,

huh Dad?" Benjie asked cheerfully as they waited in traffic, trying to get to the packed municipal parking lot.

"Guess so," Mr. Malloy said, not so cheerfully. "Why don't we go someplace else instead?"

"I want cotton candy!" Max protested immediately.

Benjie added, "Yeah, and fried bread dough. You promised."

Mr. Malloy sighed and agreed, "So I did," and inched the car forward. Finally, they made it to the parking lot.

As soon as they had made the long hot walk from the car to the park, Max announced that he had to go to the bathroom.

Mitzi's father grimly led him off to the long line in front of the blue Porta Potties, after warning Mitzi and Benjie not to budge while he was gone.

Mitzi plunked down on the low stone wall under a tree to wait.

Benjie scrambled on top of it and began walking back and forth, his arms held straight out from his sides like he was a circus performer on the high wire.

"I wish they'd hurry up," he commented after only a minute or two. "I need some chow."

"Don't say 'chow,' " Mitzi said irritably. "It

sounds so stupid. Rascal Timmons says 'chow.' "

"Geez, what's wrong with you today?" Benjie asked, balancing above her on the wall.

"What do you mean, what's wrong with me? Nothing's wrong with me."

"See? That's what I mean. You jump all over me for just asking you a question, for just being a nice brother."

Mitzi scowled and folded her arms in front of her.

Out of the corner of her eye, she saw Benjie place his heels right at the edge of the wall, then start reeling his arms wildly as if he were losing his balance.

Mitzi sighed.

Benjie fell backward onto the grass, then popped up beside her. "I'm going to be an excellent stunt man," he said.

"Yeah, right."

"You can come and visit me when I'm a big star living in Hollywood."

"Stunt men aren't big stars."

"Sure they are. Look at Gene Kenner. Look at Calvin Dunwood."

"Who are *they*?"

Benjie rolled his eyes. "Famous stunt men," he said, like she should have known.

Mitzi rolled her eyes at him in return, and shook her head.

"Think he's coming back?" Benjie asked, sitting next to her on the wall and kicking his sneakers against it rhythmically.

"What? Who?"

"Dad."

"Of course he's coming back. Didn't you see how long the bathroom line was? It's going to be awhile."

"That's not what I meant."

"Oh," Mitzi said, realizing what he was getting at. She hesitated, then asked cautiously, "Do *you* think he is?"

Benjie shrugged. "Maybe he wants to, but Mom doesn't want him to."

"Or maybe Mom wants him to, but he doesn't want to."

"Maybe." Benjie bit his bottom lip, a habit he'd had as a toddler, whenever he was scared or overtired.

Mitzi hadn't seen him do it in years. And just watching that one little action made her feel an unexpected and overwhelming sense of protectiveness.

After all, Benjie *was* still her little brother. And he was the only person in the world who knew what was going on at their house—well, besides Max, who was too little to really understand it.

"Don't you wish things were back the way they used to be?" Mitzi asked Benjie, feeling suddenly like they were a team.

"Yeah. I do."

"Me, too."

"But I don't think things are ever going to go back to the way they were."

"You don't?" Mitzi looked at him in surprise. "How come?"

He shrugged. "It's going be just like what happened with Rascal's parents. They're going to get divorced, and we're only going to see Dad on Sundays, just like Rascal only sees his father on Sundays. I know they're going to get divorced."

"How do you know?"

"I just do."

"Maybe they won't. Maybe they'll get back together."

"It doesn't seem like they're planning to."

"Well, maybe something will happen and they'll realize that they should stay married."

He snorted. "Oh, yeah, sure. Like what?"

Mitzi debated telling him about her plan. And for an instant, she even considered asking him to run away with her. Maybe losing *two* kids would make her parents get back together twice as fast . . .

Then Benjie sighed, got up, flipped over, and started balancing on his hands on the stone wall.

And Mitzi thought, *what am I, crazy?*

She pictured her brother doing a handstand

on the railing at the top of the Empire State building, or leaping from car to car on top of a speeding subway train.

No way.

As scared as she was about going to New York City alone, there was absolutely no way she was going to bring Benjie along.

She sighed, wishing this whole thing was just over.

Chapter Nine

Mitzi opened her bedroom door a crack and peeked out into the hallway. It was dark and quiet. A narrow band of yellow light spilled from beneath her parents'—her *mother's*—bedroom door, and she could hear the television faintly behind it. She knew her mother was in bed, wearing her nightshirt, watching some movie of the week.

Her brothers were in bed, too. She'd heard her mother bring them up awhile ago. Max had been worried about sleeping in the same room with Benjie, who had thrown up in the middle of the living room rug right after their father dropped them off.

Of course, Mrs. Malloy had blamed it on Mr. Malloy. "What did he feed you today?" she demanded, after settling a still-green Benjie on the couch with a pillow and some ginger ale.

"He ate fried dough, a snow cone, cotton candy, a sausage-and-onion sandwich, pizza, and some onion rings," Max said helpfully, looking up from the television program he'd been watching.

Mitzi gave him a little kick to shut him up, but Max, oblivious, only added, "Oh, yeah, and a DoveBar."

"You'd think he would know better," Mrs. Malloy said, down on her hands and knees, furiously scrubbing the rug with white foam.

"I know," Mitzi said, "I *told* him he shouldn't go around doing handstands and cartwheels after eating all that stuff. No wonder he threw up."

"I *meant* your father," Mrs. Malloy had said. "And as soon as I finish cleaning up this mess, I'm going to give him a call."

Uh-oh, Mitzi had thought. She'd escaped to her room, but even from upstairs, she could hear her mother shouting angrily into the phone.

Now, as she pushed her bedroom door open carefully, so it wouldn't creak and give her away, she felt a little flicker of doubt.

What if her plan didn't work? What if she rode the stupid bus all the way to New York City, spent a couple of nights sleeping on a hard bench, blew all of her savings, and her parents *still* got divorced?

That won't happen, she reassured herself, tiptoeing back into her room to get her duffel out of the closet.

But as she lugged the bag, which weighed a ton, onto her shoulder and snuck back to the door, she couldn't help wondering if she was about to make a huge mistake.

She was feeling overwhelmed by the urge to just forget the whole thing, to stay here and deal with whatever happened. It was so strong that she imagined that she heard a voice in her head, warning her, "Don't go! Don't do it!"

But she fought it, told it firmly, "I *have* to."

If she didn't save her parents' marriage, who would?

Come on. It's now or never.

Squaring her shoulders and adjusting her weight to carry the heavy bag, Mitzi stepped out into the hallway.

After only a moment's hesitation, she closed her door quietly behind her, then crept down the stairs and out into the moonless night.

The streets of Somerset looked a lot different after dark, when you were alone, walking. Normally, Mitzi felt reassured by the big, old-fashioned houses and sprawling trees that lined each block in the "historic district" that lay between her house and downtown.

But tonight, the houses, with their peaks and turrets, seemed spooky, even sinister. And it didn't take much imagination for Mitzi to decide that the trees that rustled above her seemed almost like looming monsters.

If she could hurry along the sidewalks at a normal pace, it wouldn't be so bad. But her bag was so impossibly heavy that she had to keep stopping to set it down for a moment, then shift it to her other shoulder. And every time she stopped, she felt like something—or someone—was going to jump out at her.

Finally, she turned the corner onto Market Street. If she went left and continued for a block, she'd be at her father's new apartment.

She went right, toward the bus terminal.

Mitzi hadn't seen another soul since she'd left her house a half hour ago, and only an occasional car had passed her. But here on Market Street, there were people, and there was traffic—well, not traffic, as in a jam, but a fairly steady stream of cars went by.

She should have been reassured by the activity, but instead, she found herself growing increasingly nervous as she headed toward the terminal. Somerset was a small town—what if someone she knew spotted her? How was she going to explain being out alone at this hour on a Sunday night, carrying luggage? What if she happened to run into her father? After all, he lived in this neighborhood, now. He could easily be out buying a quart of milk or renting a movie or something.

And on top of those possibilities, she had to deal with the fact that downtown Somerset was kind of—well, sleazy. She'd never realized that before, not when she was with her parents, or even when she was alone, in broad daylight.

But now that she was here by herself at night, she kept noticing people who seemed a little too creepy for comfort. Like the old man who sat on the steps of the post office building, clutching a paper bag and talking to himself. And the group of long-haired teenagers huddled under a street lamp. And the bikers who roared by and shouted obscenities at two women who were walking to their car in the municipal lot.

Mitzi pretended to ignore everything around her. She kept her head down as she walked, struggling to keep up her pace despite the weight of her bag. Finally, she glimpsed the bus terminal a few doors up.

It wasn't really much more than a tiny storefront, really, sandwiched between the Somerset Diner and a little corner bar that changed owners—and names—about once a year.

Right now, the place was called the C'mon Inn, according to the neon sign in the window. And there were two shifty-eyed men loitering in the doorway. Mitzi could feel their eyes on her as she passed, which sent chills prickling down her neck.

A few more steps, though, and she reached the bus terminal. At last.

The little room was empty except for the bearded, tired-looking man behind the counter, and a gray-haired man who was hanging around, chewing on a toothpick and talking to him. They both turned and looked at Mitzi as she pushed through the door and deposited her bag on the floor with a thud.

"Can I help you?" the man behind the counter asked gruffly, over the scratchy country music that blared from a small radio behind him.

"One ticket to New York City, please," she said, and thought that her voice sounded small and high-pitched, not at all like it usually did.

It struck her that the man might not let her buy a ticket by herself. What if there was some law that kids had to be accompanied by an adult? Her whole plan would fall through . . . although, the thought of going back home to her safe, cozy bedroom wasn't an altogether unappealing idea.

But the man behind the counter didn't blink an eye at the thought of her going to New York City by herself. "Next bus is at ten-fifty," he told her. "Gets into Port Authority at ten of two. That the one you want?"

She cleared her throat. "Yes," she said, trying to sound self-assured, even as she stifled a yawn. Hopefully she could sleep on the bus.

"Round trip?" he asked, puffing out a cloud of cigar smoke and opening a drawer.

She hesitated. She hadn't thought of that. Would her parents come down and pick her up? Or would she take the bus back home? What if she bought a round-trip ticket, and then didn't use it? Why waste the money?

"One way," she said decisively. She could always get a return ticket later if she needed to.

A few seconds later, she was holding a bus ticket, and the man behind the counter was tucking her money into the drawer.

"You got about forty-five minutes until the bus gets here," he said, looking up at her. Then he turned to his friend, who was still leaning and chewing on the toothpick, and went back to his conversation.

Mitzi looked around. There was a bench a few feet away, in front of the window. But half of it was covered in newspapers, and the other half looked sticky. She reached down gingerly and touched it.

Yick. It *was* sticky.

She couldn't sit here. But she was too tired to stand. There was a park bench outside on the street, but she remembered those two men in front of the bar next door, and decided she didn't want to go out there alone, either.

As she stood hesitating in the tiny, smoky bus terminal, something amazing happened.

The door opened, and Maddie walked in.

For a moment, Mitzi thought she was seeing things. How could Maddie, of all people, be here, of all places, right now, of all times?

"Hi, Mitzi," Maddie said. "Wow, what a surprise, meeting you here."

But something fleeting in her eyes told Mitzi that she wasn't all that surprised, for some reason. Before Mitzi could examine the expression, it was gone, and Maddie's clear sky-blue eyes were just sparkling and friendly, as they always were.

The two men at the counter glanced over only briefly before going back to their conversation.

"So what's up?" Maddie asked conversationally. "Going somewhere?"

"Uh, yeah. It's kind of, um . . . well . . . What are *you* doing here?" she asked, instead. She noticed that Mitzi was dressed casually and comfortably as usual, in a big T-shirt, baggy jeans that were so faded they were almost white, and her usual pair of spotless canvas sneakers.

"I was just passing by, and I happened to look in the window and saw you standing here."

"Oh."

"What time does your bus leave?"

"Ten-fifty."

"Where to?"

"New York."

Maddie just nodded. Mitzi knew she should offer some explanation. After all, she was supposed to be at Maddie's house first thing tomorrow morning to wash windows. But she couldn't seem to get out more than staccato phrases.

"Well, what time is it now?" Maddie asked.

Mitzi checked her watch. "Ten-oh-five."

"Come on, let's go over to the diner for some hot chocolate or something. I'm starved. My treat."

"Okay," Mitzi agreed, because she didn't know what else to do. Too many different emotions were colliding in her brain.

Relief at the sight of a familiar face . . .

Panic because she had been found out . . .

Confusion because she wasn't sure what to tell Maddie . . .

Suspicion because Maddie's appearance seemed too coincidental—but what else could it be?

"Is that your bag?" Maddie asked, nudging the nylon duffel with her toe.

"Oh . . . um, yeah." Mitzi bent to grab the strap, but Maddie beat her to it.

"Careful, it's—" Mitzi broke off and watched in amazement as Maddie effortlessly threw the bag over her shoulder, as though it contained nothing more than some feathers, a bag of marshmallows, and a few helium balloons.

"You don't have to carry that for me," Mitzi told her.

Maddie shrugged. "It's no problem. You've been carrying it around long enough."

How did she know? Mitzi wondered. Had Maddie followed her from home?

Oh, please. Why on earth would she have done that? Mitzi decided that her imagination sure was on overdrive tonight.

"Come on," Maddie said, leading the way to the door.

And there was nothing for Mitzi to do but follow her.

Chapter Ten

The Somerset Diner had been around forever. Mitzi's parents had come here when they were kids, and supposedly, her Grandma and Grandpa Malloy had even had their first date here.

It was a small, old-fashioned place that had a row of booths opposite the long counter lined with worn red-vinyl-topped silver stools. There were metal-topped glass sugar dispensers and napkin holders on every table. The waitresses wore pink uniforms with white aprons and most of them called everyone "hon'."

Mitzi and Maddie settled into a booth in front of the big plate-glass window and studied menus.

"I'm having hot chocolate and a bowl of cookies-'n-cream ice cream," Maddie announced. "How about you?"

Mitzi hesitated. She was too distracted to be hungry, but she decided to order something anyway. No use making Maddie suspicious. "I guess I'll have a float," she told Maddie.

"What kind?"

"Vanilla ice cream and root beer."

"Sounds yummy," Maddie said, and twirled a strand of hair around her finger.

You'd think the two of them met every Sunday night at the diner, the way Maddie was acting. Mitzi wondered why she was being so casual. She felt half grateful, and half skeptical. She couldn't seem to shake the feeling that Maddie was up to something.

But what could it possibly be? She couldn't come up with any possible explanation for Maddie to have shown up accidentally-on-purpose tonight.

It's just you, she told herself. *Stop being paranoid.*

The waitress appeared, wearing a name tag that said "Lena," and took their orders.

"So you're going to New York," Maddie said after Lena had left. It was half a question, half a comment.

"Yeah," Mitzi told her, tracing a crack in the Formica tabletop with her pinky fingernail.

"Business or pleasure?" Maddie asked, and Mitzi looked up sharply to see that she was smiling.

"Neither," she replied, staring back down at the table. She knew she had to say something more—but what? She couldn't tell Maddie the truth . . .

But she did.

For some reason, when she opened her mouth again, it came spilling out.

"I'm actually running away for a few days so that my parents will get back together."

Was that me? Did I actually say that? she wondered frantically.

She glanced at Maddie, expecting to see . . . what? Disapproval? Pity? Amusement?

But to Mitzi's surprise, the only expression on Maddie's face was one of understanding, and she was nodding. "I tried that," she told Mitzi.

"You *did?*"

"Sure."

"You're kidding. *You* ran away from home?"

"So that my parents would get back together. Yup," Maddie told her, bobbing her head up and down so that her hair bounced. "It was right after they separated. I thought that if they were worried about me, they would turn to each other for support and realize that they shouldn't split up after all."

"Did it work?" Mitzi asked, an instant before she remembered that Maddie's mother lived here in Somerset and her father lived on a houseboat in the Florida Keys.

"Nope," Maddie told her matter-of-factly. "Not only did it not work, but I got into major trouble. They grounded me for six months—my punishment was the first and only thing they've agreed on since the split."

"Oh," Mitzi said dully.

"And on top of *that*, running away was a real nightmare."

"Why?"

"Because it was dangerous. I was nearly kidnapped by a man with a gun, and I was robbed while I was sleeping in a bus station, and I had to go to the police for help, and . . ." She shuddered.

"Are you serious?" Mitzi asked, staring at her. Kidnapped? Robbed? She hadn't thought of that. But she remembered the creepy way the men out in front of the bar down the street had looked at her, and shuddered inside. And this was only Somerset.

"Yeah, it wasn't a good experience," Maddie said, shaking her head. "But hopefully, it'll turn out better for you. Maybe your parents will even get back together again, for awhile."

"For awhile?"

"Well, you have to admit, Mitzi, that if they're going to split, they're going to split. Nothing you do is going to stop them."

"Okeydokey, here we go, girls," Lena said, appearing suddenly with a tray. She set a foamy mug of cocoa and a frosty silver bowl of ice cream in front of Maddie, and a frothy float in a tall ridged glass in front of Mitzi.

"Thanks," Maddie said.

Mitzi could only nod at the waitress. As soon as Lena had gone again, she said to Maddie, "Maybe it didn't work for you, with your parents, but every situation is different. My parents are making a big mistake, and they need to realize it."

Maddie shrugged. "Maybe."

Mitzi checked her Swatch and was surprised to see that it was only a quarter after. It felt like they'd been sitting here much longer than ten minutes.

"You know," Maddie said, after swallowing a mouthful of ice cream, "you could be right. I mean, your parents might be miserable apart."

"Yeah," Mitzi said, sipping her float.

"So, are they?"

"Are they what?"

"Miserable," Maddie said, spooning more ice cream into her mouth.

"Oh." Mitzi thought about it.

Were they miserable?

She thought about her mother whistling down the hall the other night. And about how her mother had acted at Frolic Island yesterday. Not exactly miserable. Kind of . . . lighthearted, actually. And these days, her voice was brighter and more bubbly, the way it used to be. And she looked different, too. Her face looked less strained, and now that Mitzi thought about it, she didn't seem to have those deep dark circles under her eyes lately, and her mouth, which had often been set in a grim, straight line, smiled more.

"Are they?" Maddie asked again, dipping her ice cream spoon into her cocoa and tasting some of the foam. "Mmmm."

"My mom isn't exactly *miserable* on the outside," Mitzi said reluctantly. "But she probably is inside. She's just trying to hide it from me and my brothers."

"Are you sure?"

"Yes," Mitzi snapped.

Maddie didn't seem to notice. "What about your dad?"

"What about him?" she asked, even though she knew. What was up with Maddie, anyway? Why did she have to be so nosy?

"Is he miserable?" Maddie asked patiently.

"Yes," Mitzi said firmly. "Just this afternoon, we were on our way to the food fest in Ridge Hills, and you should have seen him. He was miserable."

But she had to admit, to herself, that sitting in traffic in hundred-degree heat wasn't exactly pleasant. And her father had bounced back remarkably well, teasing them and joking around all afternoon. When Max had dropped his ice cream onto his father's shoes, Mr. Malloy had just laughed, wiped them off with some spit and a napkin, and bought another cone.

No, her father wasn't exactly miserable these days, either.

But she wasn't about to admit that to Maddie.

"My parents are so much happier when they're apart," Maddie said casually. "It's amazing. When they were together, before the split, all they did was fight. It got so bad that I dreaded my father coming home from work every night, because I was afraid there would be a big battle. And there always was. You know what I mean, huh?"

Mitzi realized she'd been nodding, and forced herself to stop. "Not really," she lied.

"Anyway, all three of us were stressed out before the divorce. Now everyone's life is better. Including mine."

"But you hardly ever get to see your dad," Mitzi pointed out. "That must be awful."

"It's not *that* awful. There are worse things that can happen, you know," Maddie said, with a strangely sad expression that was gone as quickly as it had arrived. "And when I do see my dad, we spend a lot of time together. And we have a lot of fun. He takes me fishing and to the beach and stuff like that. Back when he lived at home, all he ever did was work or fight with my mom."

Mitzi thought about how much fun she and her brothers had been having on their Sunday outings with their father.

Then she pushed the thought away and checked her watch again. It was only ten-twenty. Again, she was surprised. It seemed a lot later. The crowd in the diner had thinned out considerably.

She tried to tune Maddie out as she talked about what her parents had been like before the divorce, and what they were like now, but she couldn't help absorbing some of it. Maddie had a way of getting her point across without being irritating, somehow.

Maddie's point seemed to be that sometimes, divorce was inevitable. But Mitzi still didn't want to buy it.

"You know what I think?" Maddie asked, spooning the last of her ice cream into her mouth. "I think that sometimes, a person has to grow up and stop thinking of what *they* want. They have to think about what's best for the other people involved."

"That's what I mean," Mitzi said, slapping her palm on the table. "I wish my parents would do that. If they would stop thinking of themselves, and think of their kids, they wouldn't be splitting up."

Maddie tilted her head. Her eyes were serious. "I didn't mean your parents, Mitzi," she said quietly. "I meant you."

"Me?" Mitzi stopped sipping the remaining drops of her soda and frowned.

"Yes. Think about it."

"If you're finished, we're about to close up, here," Lena announced, materializing just then at their booth.

Mitzi glanced at her watch. "I didn't know you closed at ten-thirty."

"We don't. We close at eleven."

"Eleven?" Mitzi stared at the waitress, then checked her watch again. "But it's only . . ."

Her voice trailed off as her gaze followed Lena's hand, which was pointing at something she hadn't noticed before. A clock on the wall. And both the big hand and the little hand were on the eleven.

Which meant . . .

"Oh, no!" Mitzi jumped up. "Is it almost eleven?"

"Five-to," Lena said.

"But my watch says ten-thirty. And I have to catch the bus to New York!"

"That went by about five minutes ago," Lena said helpfully. "I saw it through the window."

"I missed my bus? But how could that happen?" Mitzi asked Maddie, who was sitting there wearing an impossible-to-read expression.

"Did your watch stop?" Maddie asked.

"No, the second hand is moving," Mitzi said, examining it. "Now what am I going to do?"

"Tough break, toots," Lena said, dropping the check on the table and going back behind the counter.

"Why don't you take the bus tomorrow?" Maddie asked.

"I can't," Mitzi said, plunking down into the booth again. "My mom is taking the day off to be with me, and she didn't know I'd been working for you, and . . . what a mess."

"Well, you don't have to worry about your job," Maddie said. "Take some time off . . . looks like you were planning to do that anyway, huh?"

Mitzi nodded guiltily.

"Listen, Mitzi, it's not the end of the world," Maddie said with a reassuring pat on Mitzi's arm. "You'll see."

She stood up and reached into her pocket, pulling out some money. "I'll go pay the bill and then I'll drive you home."

There was nothing for Mitzi to do but agree.

"Well?" Maddie asked Justin.

"Good job," he said admiringly.

"I was brilliant, wasn't I," Maddie gloated.

"You were. The watch was a nice touch."

"I thought so, too." She opened her hand and added, "And look at this."

"What is it?" Justin asked, peering at the white envelope and the small, printed cardboard rectangle of cardboard.

"A one-way bus ticket to New York, and the rest of her money. Just in case."

"You pickpocketed her?"

Maddie shrugged. "I had to. I'm not proud of it, but an angel has to do whatever it takes, right, Justin?"

"Right."

"You don't think that they'll hold it against me when they decide whether I get my wings, do you?"

"What? That you stole Mitzi's money and ticket? And that you lied?" He shrugged.

"Lied?" Maddie's eyebrows went up. "When did I lie?"

"When you told Mitzi about how you were robbed and nearly kidnapped when you ran away . . . which I happen to know never happened."

"You know I was never robbed or nearly kidnapped?"

"And that you never ran away," Justin told her.

"You really were with me every step of the way while I was living, weren't you, Justin?" The idea warmed her.

"I sure was. Just like you are for Mitzi."

Maddie smiled and nodded, then peeked down at Mitzi, who was safely sound asleep in her own bedroom.

Chapter Eleven

On Monday morning, Mitzi woke up, looked around her cluttered, familiar, sun-splashed bedroom and felt relieved. Sleeping on a bench in Port Authority no longer seemed like such a great idea. Neither did running away.

Her mother knocked on her door and called, "Mitzi? You up?"

"Yeah," she croaked out in her morning voice, then cleared her throat.

The door opened and her mother poked her head in. "I just dropped the boys off at day camp. I'm going to have another quick cup of coffee while you get ready, and then we'll hit the road, Jack."

Hit the road, Jack. Her mother always used to say that when Mitzi was younger. And if Benjie was around, he would always look puzzled and ask, "Who's Jack?" And then Mitzi and her mom would grin at each other.

"I only need about twenty minutes," Mitzi said, stretching and sitting up.

Her mother nodded, started to leave, and then stopped short. Mitzi saw that she was staring at something on the floor. She propped herself up on her elbows and looked over the edge of the bed to see what it was.

Her navy blue bag was lying right in the middle of the room, where she'd dumped it last night. She'd been too tired to unpack it—so tired she barely remembered crawling into bed.

"What's that?" her mother asked, looking from the bag to Mitzi.

"It's . . ." What was she supposed to say? "It's my duffel bag," she offered brightly. "The one Aunt Lisa and Uncle Josh gave me last Christmas."

"I know *what* it is," her mother said, coming all the way into the room. "I meant, *why* is it out? And what's in it?"

"Just some stuff," Mitzi said vaguely.

"For what?"

Her mother obviously wasn't going to let her off the hook. She took a deep breath, and said, "I was going to go someplace. But then . . . I changed my mind."

There was a pause. Then her mom said

evenly, "I see. And where were you going to go?"

"New York," Mitzi said in a small voice.

"New *York?* By yourself?"

"Well, I . . . um . . . yes."

There was another pause. Mitzi watched her mother's face. It didn't look like she was about to explode and start yelling, exactly . . . more like she didn't know *what* to do.

And Mitzi knew she couldn't tell her the rest of it. About Maddie, and the job. Her mother would freak out if she knew Mitzi had been working every day, for a total stranger.

Finally, Mrs. Malloy sat on the edge of the bed and said, "You were going to run away, Mitzi? Because of your father and me?"

"Why would you think I would do that?"

"Because you obviously haven't been happy ever since Dad moved out. You've been up here in your room most of the time, and I've been worrying about you. We both have."

"You and Dad?"

"Yes."

"You've talked to Dad about me?" Mitzi asked, surprised.

Her mother looked surprised that she would be surprised. "Of course. About you, and your brothers, and—other things."

"When? And . . . where?"

"We've had lunch a few times. And I've gone over to his apartment, and—"

"You went to his *apartment?*" Mitzi couldn't believe it.

"Uh huh." Her mother made a face. "Not very . . . modern, is it?"

"It's a dump," Mitzi said, then got back to the point. "I'm really surprised."

"Why?"

"I thought you and Dad didn't want to see each other anymore, or talk, or . . . you know."

"Mitzi," her mother said, shaking her head, "No matter what kind of problems your father and I have in our marriage, we're still both responsible for you, and for your brothers. Dad might not be living here at home right now, but he still cares about us—*all* of us. And—"

"Are you trying to work things out?" Mitzi interrupted, sitting up excitedly.

"We're trying, yes. But don't get your hopes up," she added quickly. "Right now, it doesn't look like Dad's going to be coming home . . . at least, not anytime soon."

"Why not? You won't let him?" Mitzi asked angrily.

"It's not that, it's—"

"He doesn't want to?"

"It's not that either, Mitzi. And please stop yelling."

She was about to let the anger that had been

building spill out, about to demand how her mother could be so selfish, how her father could be so selfish . . .

And then she saw the tears in her mother's eyes.

"Mom?" she asked quietly, feeling her own eyes filling up. "I'm sorry. I don't mean to yell. I just . . . I wish things could go back to the way they used to be, when you and Dad were happy together."

Her mother's answer wasn't what she'd expected. "So do I."

"You do?"

Her mother nodded sadly.

And Mitzi realized that this was complicated—way more complicated than she'd ever thought.

Maddie's words echoed in her head.

Sometimes, a person has to grow up and stop thinking of what they want. They have to think about what's best for the other people involved.

Ever since her parents had split up, Mitzi had only been thinking of herself—of how it was affecting her. She hadn't stopped to think about how her parents felt. She hadn't cared.

She'd thought it was so simple—that if they wanted to work things out, they could.

But maybe they couldn't, no matter how hard they tried.

"Do you still love Dad?" she asked softly, and her mother nodded. "And he still loves you?"

"Yes," her mother said, nodding again. "But it's not that easy."

"I know."

Now it was her mother's turn to look surprised. "You do?"

"Yes. I do now," Mitzi said, and hesitated for a moment. "And Mom, I want you and Dad to be happy. Together. But if you can't be happy together, then . . . well, whatever happens, I guess will have to be okay with me."

"Oh, Mitzi . . ." Her mother hugged her, and she was enveloped in the familiar mom scent of perfume and shampoo and coffee. "When did you grow up?"

"Just now," she said honestly. *Thanks to Maddie.*

Tuesday night after supper, Mitzi decided to walk down to the mailbox at the end of the street to mail the letter she'd just written to Nikki. She'd told her all about her shopping trip with her mother yesterday, and about how they'd gone out to lunch today.

And she'd told her other things, too. About her parents splitting up. After all, she couldn't pretend it would go away if she didn't admit it. It had actually felt good getting it down on paper. Maybe she would even call Nikki at camp one of these days, to talk . . .

"Hey, Millicent, where ya going?"

She rolled her eyes and kept walking.

Rascal Timmons rode up beside her on his bike. "Mailing a letter?" he asked, apparently spotting the envelope in her hand.

"What does it look like, Hulbert?" She picked up her pace.

"Hey, what were you doing in the diner the other night?" Rascal asked, causing her to stop walking and stare at him in surprise.

"What diner?" she asked, narrowing her eyes.

"*Duh*," he said, making an idiot face at her and braking his bike next to her. "The Somerset Diner. What other diner is there?"

"How do you know I was there?"

"Because I was out with my dad, at the movies. Boy, was my mom mad that he didn't get me home until almost eleven!"

Mitzi nodded. Rascal's mother was always having big blowups with her ex-husband. The whole neighborhood could usually hear them shouting at each other on Sundays when Mr. Timmons came to pick Rascal up or drop him off.

"Anyway," Rascal continued, "we were walking down Market Street on the way to the car afterward, and I looked in the window of the diner and saw you."

"Oh." She wasn't about to tell Rascal the real story, so she just said, "I was meeting a friend. She was upset about something and she needed to talk to someone."

"What friend?"

"Maddie. You don't know her."

"Yeah, well I didn't see her, either."

"What do you mean, you didn't see her? She was with me at the diner."

He shrugged. "When I saw you, you were alone."

"I was not alone. I was with Maddie."

"Didn't see her," Rascal said in a maddeningly confident voice.

"Well, you must not have been wearing your glasses, then, *Hulbert*. Because she was there with me the whole time."

"Whatever you say, Millicent." He started pedaling his bike again, making a loop around her and heading back toward home. "Wait'll I tell Benjie."

"Tell Benjie what?" she called after him.

"That you have an imaginary friend," Rascal said, and snickered as he rode away.

Mitzi stood on the sidewalk, watching him and frowning.

He's just giving you a hard time, she told herself. *You know how Rascal is.*

But she couldn't help feeling faintly uneasy, anyway.

Oh, well. Tomorrow morning she was going to go back to Maddie's. And suddenly, she couldn't wait to see her again.

It was just past eight-thirty when Mitzi turned onto Grimby Manor Wednesday morning. The sky was overcast today, and rain was forecast. The trees were rustling above her head, their leaves turning up the way they did when a storm was on the way.

Mitzi would have to put her bike on the porch while she was at Maddie's so it wouldn't get wet.

She was going to be there awhile. Not only did she want to help with the window washing, but she had quite a few things to tell Maddie. First, of course, she would tell her that she couldn't work anymore. She didn't want to keep sneaking around behind her mother's back, and besides, she suddenly felt like she wanted to stick closer to home.

But she would tell Maddie what had happened with her parents—how, thanks to Maddie, she now understood about not being selfish, and accepting things that happened, even when they weren't the greatest.

And she would tell Maddie that even though

she couldn't work for her mom anymore, she still wanted to be friends. Because that was what she considered Maddie, more than anything else. A friend.

As usual, Grimby Manor was deserted. But as Mitzi rode along toward the end of the block, she couldn't help feeling like something was different. Something wasn't quite right . . .

Just before she reached the familiar iron fence that bordered Maddie's house, she passed a woman who was out walking her dog.

The dog had stopped to sniff the grass along the curb, and the woman was hurrying it along, saying, "Come on, now, Gidget, you don't want us to get caught in the rain, now, do you?"

Mitzi pedaled past Gidget and her mistress, aware that both were studying her curiously, and arrived in front of the tall iron fence.

She hopped off her bike, glanced toward the gate, and froze.

The gate was closed.

And that wasn't all.

Beyond the fence, the hedges and trees suddenly seemed straggly and overgrown.

It's just because it's a gloomy day, Mitzi told herself, putting her kickstand down and walking slowly toward the gate. *And Maddie probably didn't leave the gate open because she didn't know I was coming. That's all.*

But that wasn't all.

She reached the gate and caught a glimpse of what lay beyond. The gardens were choked with weeds and the lawn was overgrown and bedraggled. The house no longer looked like a gingerbread confection—it looked like a haunted, abandoned place that should have a "condemned" sign nailed to the front door. Gone were the many shades of pink paint and the flowers in the window boxes. The scalloped shingles were a nondescript, gray-beige color, some of them missing altogether, and a few of the windows were broken.

The whole place looked desolate and deserted.

"Excuse me, are you looking for someone?"

Mitzi turned slowly and saw that the lady and Gidget were standing beside her.

"My friend Maddie," she said hopefully. "She lives here."

The woman looked startled. "She can't live here," she said, shaking her head at the old house and wrapping another length of Gidget's leash around her hand. "No one has in years."

"But . . ."

"It's such a shame," the woman went on, as Gidget sniffed around Mitzi's shoes. "The place could be gorgeous if someone would just buy it and fix it up. Right now, it's an eyesore—was that a drop?"

"What?" Mitzi asked vacantly.

The woman held out her hand, palm outstretched, and looked at the sky. "That *was* a drop," she announced. "I just felt another one. It's raining. Come on, Gidget." She tugged on the leash.

Mitzi just stood watching as the woman and her dog hurried away.

Then she turned back and looked at the house again as the rain started to come down harder.

"Where are you, Maddie?" she whispered bleakly. "Did I imagine you?"

There was no other explanation. Rascal Timmons must have been right. She had created an imaginary friend, someone to help her through a rough time.

"But you seemed so real," she said aloud. "All of it did—the job, and baking cookies together, and the other night at the diner . . ."

She sighed, got slowly on her bike, and rode toward home.

Epilogue

"Maddie? Are you crying?" Justin asked, popping in.

"Kind of," she said, wiping her eyes.

"What's wrong?"

"I was just watching Mitzi. She thinks I wasn't real. And before long, she's going to forget all about me."

"She's supposed to," Justin said. "Just like you forgot all about me. But you'll see her again someday."

"Not until January 16, 2079. She's not scheduled to show up here until then."

"Well, time flies when you're in heaven. You'll see."

"Heaven?" ~~Mitzi~~ Maddie asked, perking up and turning to look at Justin. "Did you say heaven?"

"Yes, I said heaven. I just got word—you made it, Maddie. You've earned your wings."

"I did? I really did? I made it!" Maddie squealed, and grabbed him in an enormous hug.

"You did a great job," Justin told her in a slightly strangled voice. "Uh, could you loosen your arms a little?"

"Oops, sorry," she said, giggling. "I'm just so psyched about heaven. Wait till I tell Nathan and Thea and Bryan." Then she thought of something, and sobered. "I *will* be able to tell them, won't I?"

"Sure," Justin said. "You can visit them in the Holding Gardens whenever you feel like it. You just can't spill any secrets . . . and you're about to learn a lot of them."

"Secrets? Like what? You mean, like whether life exists in other galaxies? And whether there's really a Loch Ness monster? Stuff like that?"

Justin was nodding. "Exactly. And all the other things you've always wondered about."

"Good. Then I can find out whatever happened to that library book I lost in third grade and had to pay for out of my allowance. It took months."

"*Charlotte's Web?*" Justin asked. "I can tell you that. Your dog carried it outside when you weren't looking and buried it in the yard under the clothesline pole."

"I should have known." Maddie shook her head. "Good old Snickers . . . I've always missed that dog. He died when I was ten."

"Well you're about to see him again," Justin said, grinning. "And everyone else, too—your great-grandparents, and your uncle Billy, and the others—they're all waiting for you."

"They are!" Maddie clutched his arm, wide-eyed. "When can we go?"

"Whenever you're ready," Justin said.

"I'm ready," she said quickly.

"All right, then . . ."

"Wait!" she said suddenly, stopping. "What about Mitzi? I still get to keep an eye on her, right?"

"Right. You're her guardian angel for the rest of her time on earth."

"Then let me take another quick peek at her," Maddie said, and Justin nodded and stepped back.

Maddie looked and quickly found Mitzi. She was in her backyard, pushing Max on the swingset while Benjie hung upside-down from his knees in a tree.

"See, you guys?" Mitzi was asking. "I *told* you it wasn't going to rain all day. I knew the sun would come out."

"She's going to be fine now," Maddie said, turning back to Justin with a contented sigh. "I'm ready to go."

"All right, come on then," he said, and started to lead her toward heaven.

"Wait!" she said again, and stopped.

"What now?" Justin asked impatiently.

"I forgot something."

"What is it?"

"This," Maddie said, and a familiar bag popped into her outstretched hand. "Okay, let's go."

And at last, Maddie went off to heaven, munching happily on cookies from her bottomless bag.

Keep an eye out for *Britany Butterfield and the Back-to-School Blues*—coming soon!

Brittany Butterfield and the Back-to-School Blues

Brittany Butterfield figures that life can't get any worse. It's bad enough that she's entering a brand-new school—where she'll be a nobody underclassman—but her two best friends aren't in *any* of her classes. Plus, *they've* got boyfriends, and Brittany doesn't. And to top it off, in gym class she feels like she has two left feet! The only *good* thing about school is the newspaper club, but Brittany's too shy to even think about joining.

Then Brittany makes a new friend. He's Nathan, a really nice guy who tries to help her overcome her shyness. His flattering attentions start to make Brittany think that maybe she's important after all. She even starts playing softball. But can she find the confidence to go after what she *really* wants—and become a writer?